Join Nancy Parker as she . . .

. . . goes **UNDERCOVER** and tests out her acting skills

. . . discovers a **DEAD BODY** and opens up her own murder investigation

. . . forms a **SECRET ALLIANCE** with an old friend

. . . is snowed in with a house full of **MURDER SUSPECTS**

. . . unearths **SECRET** passages, **SHOCKING** rumours, and double-crossing **IMPOSTERS!**

For Our Dear Little Archie

NANCY PARKER'S

Chilling Conclusions

MAIDSERVANTS, MYSTERY
AND MURDER!

OXFORD

UNIVERSITY PRESS

Great Clarendon Street, Oxford OX2 6DP

Oxford University Press is a department of the University of Oxford.
It furthers the University's objective of excellence in research, scholarship,
and education by publishing worldwide. Oxford is a registered trade mark
of Oxford University Press in the UK and in certain other countries

First published 2018

British Library Cataloguing in Publication Data

Data available

ISBN: 978-0-19-274699-3

1 3 5 7 9 10 8 6 4 2

Printed in Great Britain

Paper used in the production of this book is a natural,
recyclable product made from wood grown in sustainable forests.
The manufacturing process conforms to the environmental
regulations of the country of origin.

NANCY PARKER'S

Chilling Conclusions

by

JULIA LEE

ILLUSTRATED BY CHLOE BONFIELD

OXFORD
UNIVERSITY PRESS

1 BUMPING INTO MISS LAMB

NANCY'S JOURNAL

If I had not argued with Grandma & then STORMED OUT I would not have walked so far. If I hadn't walked so far I would not have bumped into Miss Lamb.

BUMPING INTO MISS LAMB CHANGED EVERYTHING!!

But I am running on too fast & must Begin at the Beginning.

We had a pretty poor Christmas at our house. Aunty Bee has been ill—which is not like her—& Grandma has been moaning—which is. Dad never says much but I could see that he was made even sadder than usual by this. Added to that I LOST MY JOB. I was helping out (again) on Mr Boyd's fruit & veg stall in the market. All very busy with the Christmas trade—then afterwards: Thank you Nancy & goodbye! Not so much as a mouldy cabbage to take home with me.

That's why I was rowing with Gran. She thinks I could

have done much more to keep the job. I know I couldn't.
Didn't want to neither. Standing in the cold all day selling
veg is miserable. But Gran says 'Ungrateful—that's what
you are!' And 'Getting above yourself.' And 'If you know
what's good for you . . . !'

But I do know what's good for me. It's time to look for
something new.

That's where Miss Lamb came in. (Tho it was PURE
CHANCE that she did.) I had almost walked off my rage at
Gran by the time I came to the far side of the Heath. From
there it is not far to the posh shops in the Vale so I decided
to carry on—see if they still had their windows decked out
for Christmas. Nothing like a fancy window dissplay to cheer
you up on a bitter-cold winter day—even if you haven't got
sixpence to your name. You can always LOOK.

So I was gazing in the Stationer's window at the new
books & pens & pencils when a voice said 'Nancy Parker!'
I turned to see Miss Lamb—all snug in a big fur collar—
along with another lady I didn't know.

(Miss Lamb is my old schoolteacher. It was her that
got me keeping a Journal. She gave me my 1st beutiful
notebook when I left school last summer on the day I
turned 14—& I've been writing ever since!)

(I am still not much good at Spelling.)

Miss L. said she often wundered what became of me.
I told her about my Journals & was just starting on my

adventures as a maidservant when the lady with her made a big show of shivering. Right—I thoght—she wants to get rid of me! But instead she said 'Let's hear Nancy's story somewhere warm. I vote we treat her to tea & buns.' (I'm glad she said TREAT cos I couldn't afford to pay.) That's how we ended up in a cozy tearoom eating toasted crumpets. The only trouble was—after the cold outside— my nose began to run! I wish my hankie had been a bit more respecktable. Gran would be cross all over again if she knew.

Miss Lamb's frend is called Miss Bowman. She called Miss Lamb 'Minta' (short for 'Araminta') and Miss Lamb called her 'Meg'. They seemed to know each other very well & kept swapping glances at some of the things I said.

Trying to act like a polite lady taking tea I asked

9

Miss Lamb for _her_ news. Turns out she is engaged to be married—to a Hospital Doctor name of James MacDonald. She wasn't wearing a ring as the news is not public yet. (Confess I didn't really know what she meant there. But what she said next explained it.) 'Before school starts again I am to visit James's grandmother—a very grand lady indeed! She wants to look me over to see if I AM SUITABLE.' Miss Lamb gave a little laugh. 'After that we can announce our engagement.'

She went on to say that the grandmother lives in a huge house down in the country & that when she invited people to stay they came with their own personal servants—valets & maids & drivers. Of course Miss Lamb—being an ordinary Schoolteacher—doesn't have any such thing.

This is where Miss Bowman began to twitch her eyebrows & make faces across the table. 'Don't you see, Minta? The answer is staring right at you!'

I wasn't sure at that point. But I had an INKLING.

'Nancy would make a perfect lady's maid' Miss Bowman went on. 'She knows how they do things in big houses. She just told us she lost her last place & has nothing else lined up.'

Then I knew _for certain_.

I've worked as a housemaid & a sort of general servant & I know how to cook a pie. But I've never done anything fancy like take care of a lady's frocks or arrange her hair. Nobody ever asked me. Till now.

They swapped more glances—Miss Bowman's eyes positively dancing—until Miss Lamb went 'Well? Could you do it Nancy?'

I am not exackly a Dab-Hand with a sewing needle nor do I have a secret method for getting grease spots out of silk. But I was THRILLED AT THE PROSPECK of helping Miss Lamb out. She was the only teacher at school who saw I had a brain in my head.

So I replied—in a v. offhand way—'I expect I could act being a lady's maid. If it's only for a day or two. Can't be that much to it.'

Then Miss Lamb really did laugh & remarked that there would be very little to it in her case as she hadn't got any really fancy clothes & always did her own hair which is just drawn back & pinned. (She does not suffer from Troublesome Frizz like me.)

I told them both that it was a dream of mine to become an Actress & this would be good experiense. Even if no one but me & Miss Lamb knew I was acting. Of course I know by now that it is vain to think I will find my No. 1 Dream Job—being A DETECTIVE—until I am older (and wiser!?). But a spot of acting may well turn out to be a right lark. And it's not as if I've anything else to do right now.

When we left the tearoom Miss Bowman gave me 5 shillings to get a new Journal. She said 'I want to read all about your next adventure & this will mean I can.' I

did not spend all the 5 bob. I went into the Stationer's &
got this—just a small black notebook—but it will do very
well. It fits in a pocket & is <u>easy to hide</u>. Which is very
important with Journals—as I have found out before to
my cost!!

2 SHERLOCK HOLMES'S DRESSING GOWN

Quentin Ives felt sick. He was slithering about in the back of his father's brand new motor car. Every time they went round a bend he slid from one side to the other of the smooth leather seat; and these country roads were all bends. Beyond the windows, snow was whirling, obscuring the view. Looking out into the swirling flakes made him feel even sicker.

Quentin's father was absolutely thrilled with the car. It was much more powerful than his old one, and he drove at speed, regardless of the snow. From time to time Mrs Ives, in the front, would pipe up, 'Really, Geoffrey! Do we have to go quite so fast?' But nothing she said made any difference.

They were on their way to somewhere called Midwinter Manor. At breakfast that morning Mr Ives had lowered his newspaper to say, 'Remind me again—why are we going?'

Mrs Ives said, 'Because Lady Sleete invited us!'

'And how is it that we know Lady Sleete?'

'*You* don't know her, Geoffrey. Not yet. She and I are

on the same charity committee.'

'Great chums, are you? First I've heard of it. Thought you said the woman was an utter nincompoop.'

Mrs Ives was always calling people nincompoops, but now she fussed about with her toast and marmalade and said, 'Not at all. Never. No. I *may*, long ago, have expressed some doubt about her capabilities, but that was before we were well-acquainted…'

Quentin watched his mother. In his expert opinion (he was modelling himself on his hero, Sherlock Holmes) she was very flattered, and rather flustered, by Lady Sleete's invitation. He could deduce all this because her nose turned pink and she blinked a lot and took random bites of her toast. He liked to spend family mealtimes—which were otherwise frantically boring—refining his observation skills. But his father made things hard by vanishing completely behind the outspread pages of *The Times*.

Deductions completed, Quentin tucked into his bacon and eggs. He was not looking forward to the trip to Midwinter Manor. If only his parents would let him stay at home! The Christmas holidays were running out fast and he didn't want to waste a single day of them on some boring visit to strangers. He had a Junior Chemistry Set to mess about with, and a stack of new books to read. All that would keep his mind off school. Quentin dreaded going back for another term. He'd got off to a bad start at boarding school last year and didn't seem to be able to make up for it. But his father wouldn't hear of him changing schools, and his mother wouldn't hear of him staying at home alone. Their housekeeper had gone away to visit family, the maid was off to her mother's as soon as breakfast was cleared, and the house would be shut up for a few days. Quentin declared that he would manage perfectly. He pictured himself feasting on turkey sandwiches and cold Christmas pudding.

'It would be like camping,' he said to his mother. 'Just, not in a tent.'

His mother refused to listen. She said, 'Lady Sleete expressly included you in the invitation. I believe there will be other children there.' A statement which made Quentin's heart sink even further. He spent far too much time cooped up with loads of other boys who were noisy, messy, rude, and occasionally smelly. Some were bullies; others were sneaks. He was fed up to the back teeth with *other children*.

Mrs Ives peered out at the heavy sky. 'Now, Quentin, be a good boy and fetch your suitcase. It's a long drive and we need to be on our way.'

Quentin hurried up to his room. If he *had* to go he would spend every minute avoiding those other children, and a good way to do that was by sticking his nose in a book. He grabbed *The Christmas Annual For Boys*, two of his new adventure books, and a handful of comics from his considerable collection.

The suitcase lay on his bed. The maid had packed it, while his mother stood by giving instructions. Quentin had not been consulted. He found it stuffed with clothes and shoes, including—ugh!—his black patent dancing slippers. There wasn't a speck of space for what *he* wanted to take. On top was a formal jacket of stiff tartan wool with a matching bow tie. His mother made him wear it to children's parties and he hated it. Below it was his new dressing gown. If he took that out he would have much more room for books, as it was big and bulky. He hesitated. The dressing gown came almost to his ankles and tied round his middle with a silk cord. When he put it on and walked up and down he felt like Sherlock Holmes pacing about at 221b Baker Street, pondering his latest puzzle. Quentin didn't smoke a pipe or play the violin, of course. But if he looked in his wardrobe mirror and squinted his eyes, he had to say that the resemblance was remarkable.

Leaving the dressing gown in place, he took out the tartan jacket and hid it in the back of his wardrobe. He flung the black patent shoes after it, and arranged his books in the gaps they left. Then he slammed the lid, clicked the locks, and heaved the case downstairs.

So now he was stuck in the back of the motor car, grumpy and nauseous. But at least he had plenty to read, and wouldn't have to look a *perfect nitwit* in patent pumps and that awful jacket.

Dear Gran, Dad, & Aunty,
Just a quick line from the
station before our train. Miss
Lamb is v. kind. Bound to
enjoy working for her. Hope
Aunty Bee's cough is getting
better. Don't worry about
me. See you after my latest
adventure!

Nancy xxx

Post Card

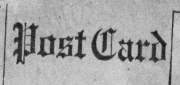

All at 44 Bread Street,
London, S.E.

3 IN THE LADIES' WAITING ROOM

NANCY'S JOURNAL

I am writing this in the Ladies Waiting Room at Waterloo Station. Miss Lamb is sitting across from me reading the newspaper. We just had a pot of tea & sausage rolls in the Tea Room. (Must say it feels A BIT ODD to be writing about someone when they could reach over to my notebook & take a look for themselves!)

Gran was not keen on me taking this job but Aunty Bee said Good Luck. So last night I stayed at Miss Lamb's & we spent the evening practissing—me at being a Lady's Maid & Miss Lamb practissing being the sort of lady who employs a lady's maid!

Miss Bowman found it all v. funny but she was helpful too. (Miss L. & Miss Bowman share the flat which is at the top of a nice old house in Blackheath.) She has lent Miss Lamb an evening dress & a necklace. Plus she sewed some lace on to a plain black frock I had from my last place in service & took the hem up a few inches—cos she said a Lady's Maid must have a bit of <u>style</u>. She had even gone to the trouble of dyeing the lace black so it was suitable.

Miss Lamb said 'Oh dear—I fear that the most unsuitable thing is ME!'

She confessed she is very nervous about meeting her fee-on-cee's grandmother. Miss Bowman said 'Nonsense. She will adore you.' But she didn't twinkle & laugh so much when she said that. (Which made my <u>detective's nose</u> begin to twitch!)

Miss Lamb replied 'I wish you were coming too Meg'—& Miss Bowman said 'You don't need <u>me</u>. You will have James by your side.' (I felt she wanted to say '<u>On</u> your side'. I am sniffing a STORY here!)

Then we made up the sofa with blankets & pillows & that's where I slept. In the morning Miss Lamb & Miss Bowman ate breakfast in their silk Dressing Gowns. Afterwards Miss Bowman went off to work—she writes for a Magazine!—& I helped Miss Lamb pack. We put tishoo paper between her frocks. According to Miss Bowman that is how you stop them creasing. Miss Lamb said 'Such a silly fuss. In a just a few hours you will be taking all this out again, Nancy—& we shall be at Midwinter Manor.' That made her sigh.

Midwinter Manor is the name of the house we are going to & its owner is called Lady Sleete. (I know how that's spelled cos I saw the Invitation: thick white card with a fancy edge. I will try & sketch it here.) Miss Lamb tells me there is a stream there called the Winterborn & it runs thru the villages of Upwinter, Midwinter & Lower Winter. Sounds very picture-esk to me. (Miss L. has never been there but got all this from Dr James.)

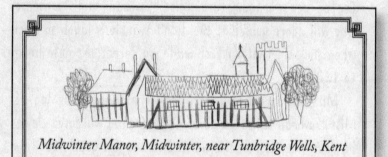

Midwinter Manor, Midwinter, near Tunbridge Wells, Kent

Lady Sleete requests the company of ...

I never heard of Lady Sleete before but seems she is Famous for bringing important people together at her dinners & parties & what-not down in the country. I keep thinking that last week I was on the Veg stall wearing Dad's old overcoat with a sack tied round my waist & tonight I will be at a grand house in my black dress with the lace on—hobnobbing with Butlers & Footmen & such—and other ladies maids. I hope they will not see thru my ACT!

Outside it's snowing but the flakes are melting as soon as they touch the ground. Miss Lamb has lent me a black wool scarf to keep out the cold but I fear my shoes are a bit leaky.

Now our train has been announced—must hurry. (Glad this notebook fits in my pocket.)

4 SO FAR SO GOOD

NANCY'S JOURNAL

At Midwinter Manor now—and So Far So Good. (I think.)
As far as I can tell nobody seemed supprised to find that
I'm here as a Lady's Maid. I think the other servants are
far too busy to give me a second glance. Phew!

Lady Sleete's driver collected Miss Lamb & me from the
station. There was another visitor off the same train—a
gentleman who must be a regular as he said 'Hello again
Betts' to the driver as he handed over his case. His name
is Jasper Grant. He inter-duced himself to Miss Lamb &
I heard her say 'THE Jasper Grant?' adding that she had
only read 2 of his books. (So he's a Writer!) He laughed in
a nice way & said that was 2 more than most people who
claimed to know all about him. Sounded to me like they'd
struck a good note right away. So maybe Miss L. needn't
have worried about this trip. Also Mr Grant had no manservant with him—just his luggage. Perhaps she got the
Wrong End of the stick about those rules too.

Course I was dying to get a good look at A Real-Life
Author but I was up front with the driver & knew I must
keep staring ahead. Good servants have to act like they
are made of stone—never Flesh & Blood—& never ever
like they've got a brain.

I should add that it is VERY SNOWY in the countryside.

By the time we got to the stop for Midwinter it was dark but I could see great heaps of snow glinting under the station lamps. And snowflakes coming down thicker than ever!

Midwinter Manor turns out to be VAST and VERY VERY OLD. The car stopped some way off & the Butler & a Footman came out with big Umbrellas to take us into the house. Turns out that's cos there is a Moat all the way round the manor. The water was black as tar. We had to walk over a footbridge & thru an archway. Then across a sort of yard—but much grander—to reach the front door. I knew my shoes really were LEAKY by that time!! Inside I got wisked away upstairs by a housemaid, & the Butler (whose name is Fortnum) ushered Miss Lamb & Mr Grant off somewhere else. Miss L. gave me one look over her shoulder & that was it. Don't know if she was saying 'Good Luck!'—or 'Help!!'

The housemaid took me up to the servants bedrooms on the top floor of the East Range. Seems I will be sharing with another girl—tho she was nowhere to be seen. (Wunder what she's like? I hope she is the frendly sort. Might pick up some useful tips off her.) The room is v. comfy compared to others I've had. No doubt cos Ladies Maids are further up the Pecking Order than the other maidservants & expected to be most refined. There was a table with sewing things on (hope nobody needs me to sew!) & a Dress-form beside it—just like a HEADLESS BODY standing on one leg! I shall have to remember that's all it is if I wake up in the middle of the night!!

Nancy's Nightmare — and not just cos of the sewing!!

The bed nearest the fireplace was already taken. I spotted a pair of shoes & a suitcase tucked underneath. Which left the one by the window for me—which is probbly more drafty. But if I got there 1st I would have nabbed the best bed too.

The housemaid waited while I left my bag & coat there & then took me off again downstairs so I could unpack for Miss Lamb. She pointed things out on the way—The Blue

Room, The Red Room, the North Range & so on. I tried to remember all the stairs & passageways & how many Right & Left turns we took so I wouldn't get lost. My last maidservant job was in a big house but nothing so vast & cumplicated as this!

Miss Lamb is staying in the Rose Room in the West Range. Her hat & coat were flung on the bed so she must have been here. I wunder if she is feeling the same as me—a bit bamboozled by everything?

The Rose Room is smaller & pokier than I expected seeing as how grand the house is. (Have the other visitors been given better rooms??) But there are silk bedcovers sewn with roses & its very own little bathroom with a Hip Bath & a rose-painted washbasin. While I was in there arranging Miss Lamb's washing things I heard voices—2 ladies chatting & laughing. Must be from the room next door. I heard one quite clearly say 'Awful bore' & the other reply 'Not for long'. Then they laughed & I heard the words '. . . won't get up to mischief' and 'whatever makes you think . . .'—goodness knows what they were on about . . . !

If the walls are that thin I must be <u>v. careful</u> nobody overhears me & Miss Lamb talking. (Wouldn't want to give the game away that I am not what I seem.)

Next I put away Miss L.'s clothes—dispite the Tishoo Paper they were creased. I laid her nightgown out ready on the bed—but it looked like a cross between a Scarecrow

& a Corpse! So I folded it up until it only looked like a nightgown again.

After that I couldn't think what else to do so sat down & wrote this Journal. I really don't know what happens next—it is all quite strange—I wonder if someone will come & fetch me? I am dying for a cup of tea!! It feels like a very long time since those sausage rolls at Waterloo.

5 OTHER CHILDREN

There *were* other children at Midwinter Manor. Quentin could hear their voices, right outside his bedroom door. They had strange accents. One said, 'Go on,' and the other, 'But—what if he's just *awful?*'

What foul cheek! Criticizing him before they'd even met him. Quentin wasn't going to stand for that. He flung open the door. A boy and a girl stood there, open-mouthed. The girl's hand was raised, about to knock.

The boy took a step backwards. 'We're Scottie and Beans Otter,' he said. He was taller than Quentin and had a head shaped like a pear drop.

'We came to say hello,' said the girl, grinning and staying put. She was much shorter, and her face was absolutely covered in freckles. 'I'm Beans. He's Scottie. Just to be clear.'

'Quentin Ives,' said Quentin gruffly. 'Wait a minute— did you say your name was Otter?'

'No need to make any jokes,' said the boy.

'Wasn't going to. Only, I know someone called Otter and it's an unusual name. Her father's an expert on archaeology. Wonder if you might know—?'

'Ella!?' they exclaimed together.

'Her father is our dad's cousin,' said Scottie, and Beans added, with a squeak of excitement, 'We were just with them in Seabourne for Christmas!'

Quentin had fond memories of Seabourne, where he had spent last summer and met Ella Otter. They'd hated each other on sight, of course, but then they got caught up in an adventure and that changed everything. Quentin didn't find it easy to make friends but being thrown together in danger really helped!

Scottie puffed out his chest. 'Our dad is Cosway Otter, the inventor. He's on a tour of Europe, looking into all kinds of manufacturing. He brought us along with him.'

Before he could stop himself Quentin said, 'That sounds frightfully dull.'

'Oh, we've seen lots of museums and cathedrals and art galleries along the way,' Beans told him.

That sounded frightfully dull, too. Like a very extended school outing.

'We're American,' Scottie declared.

Which explained their accents. His Sherlock Holmesian powers of deduction must have deserted him for a moment. That horrid motor car journey had shaken him up so much that he couldn't think straight. He gave his head a quick shake and vowed to pay more attention.

'Miss Kettle asked us to show you around Midwinter Manor,' Beans went on. 'Are you ready?'

Quentin glanced down at his front. He was wearing his smartest white shirt with a school tie. His mother was very keen that he make a *good impression*. No doubt she'd like him to wear the ridiculous tartan jacket. Little did she know that it was still at home.

'Oh, quite ready,' Quentin said airily. He had no idea who Miss Kettle was, but he wasn't about to let on. 'Are *you*?'

Both Otter children nodded. They wore lumpy knitted sweaters, Scottie's a startling green with red cuffs, Beans's egg-yellow with a blue stripe round the waist: the sort of thing you'd wear for climbing trees and mucking about in streams. Quentin couldn't help looking down to see if they had wellington boots on. They didn't, but both pairs of shoes badly needed a polish. That must mean that their father either didn't notice, or didn't care about impressing anyone. It was unlikely that their mother was on the trip with them, unless she was blind or something. Pleased with his deductions, Quentin said, 'Lead the way, then. This house is an absolute maze. I shall never find my way about.'

'You just have to remember,' said Beans, 'that basically it's a square, with the courtyard in the centre. That means there's a North side, a South side, an East side and a—'

Scottie interrupted her. 'He can probably work out the rest.'

Quentin saw Beans stick her tongue out at her brother's back, just as Scottie turned away. He couldn't help but smile.

6 A GAME OF MARBLES

Scottie and Beans went down the twisting staircase, their heads craning at each turn, their eyes taking in every inch of the panelled walls as they passed.

Quentin followed them down. With a superior air, he remarked, 'I don't suppose you've been in an actual castle before.'

'We stayed in a *schloss* in Germany,' said Beans.

'And several *chateaux* while we were in France,' Scottie added. 'Remember the one that had so many towers it looked like a clump of toadstools growing out of a log?'

Beans laughed. 'Also,' she pointed out for Quentin's benefit, 'Midwinter Manor isn't a castle. It's called a moated house. Miss Kettle filled us in on its history.'

'Begun around 1320 with the wing now called the East Range—' Scottie chanted. 'We've been here since yesterday, so we got a head start on you.'

They came to a heavy carved door and stopped.

'Should we—?' Beans asked, and Scottie answered with just the smallest shake of his head. Yet despite that, after listening at the door for a few moments, they opened it and stepped inside. Quentin was on their heels. He found their manner strange and rather irritating. Perhaps that was how brothers and sisters behaved, though. He wouldn't know, being an only child himself; and that's how he liked it.

'The Library!' announced Scottie. It was a long room lit by harsh white light reflecting off the snow outside. Windows on the left-hand side looked out over the moat and on the right into the courtyard. All down the room were bays of bookshelves, and there were *two* fireplaces, one at each end. Quentin tried to think when he had ever been in a grander room, and couldn't. In front of him stretched a highly-polished wooden floor: the ideal place for Sherlock Holmes to pace up and down and *cogitate*.

'This room has the perfect floor for a game of marbles,' said Beans, crouching on one knee and opening a small cloth bag. She tipped several glass marbles into her palm. Scottie stayed standing, hands in pockets, gazing about the room.

'I thought we were going exploring,' Quentin said.

'Oh, we *are*,' Scottie murmured back.

'Not if we're going to stop and—'

'Hush,' said Beans, in a way which Quentin felt was utterly infuriating from someone smaller and probably younger than him, and *a girl*, at that. He estimated that Scottie was at least thirteen and Beans was only ten or eleven. Quentin himself was twelve and a quarter.

'*Shall* we tell him, Scottie?' Beans went on. She was rolling marbles along the floorboards. Quentin heard one click against the next.

Scottie strolled from one bay of bookshelves to the next, staring hard at the woodwork rather than the books. He said, 'I guess so. Miss Kettle will probably say something anyhow.'

Quentin exploded. 'Look, what *is* all this shall-we, shan't-we?! It really is awfully annoying, you know. And who's this Miss Kettle you keep talking about?'

He found two pairs of round grey eyes staring back at him in surprise.

Scottie spoke in a calm, slightly patronizing, tone. 'Miss Kettle is Lady Sleete's companion—an unpaid assistant, as I understand it—and she's been given the task of overseeing us kids.'

'*Younger visitors,*' Beans corrected him. 'She said we should stick together. Have some fun.'

Scottie added, 'So we'd better tell.'

Beans explained. 'When Miss Kettle explained Midwinter Manor's history, she said we might look out for several curious things. You see, the house is so old, and was built over so many centuries, that past owners were able to make secret chambers within its walls.'

'Secret chambers?' Quentin's mood began to improve.

'Yes! They're said to be hidden behind sliding panels and fake walls. There are passageways they could use as escape routes so that people in danger could get away.'

Scottie interrupted his sister to add, in a superior tone, 'Not always escape routes. Some were built so that the Lord of the Manor could *spy* on his visitors. If a rival or an enemy came to call, their party would be shown into a room where he could overhear them without their knowledge. He'd keep them waiting for ages so they'd be bound to talk amongst themselves, in the hope that he'd hear something useful—something he could use against them. It was all very cunning.'

Beans stepped close to Quentin and lowered her voice. Her eyes were dancing. 'And we've found a secret chamber! Or at least, we found a panel that opens, though we've only managed to stick our heads inside so far.'

'Of course it may just be a cupboard. It's in Dad's bedroom.' Scottie was running his fingertips over some wooden panelling. 'Which is right above this library. So if there's a passage it could lead down here.'

'We came to search,' Beans whispered, 'but we don't want anyone catching us at it. Then it wouldn't be secret any more.'

Scottie laughed, and moved on to the next piece of wall. 'Miss Kettle mentioned that *roundels* were the supposed to be the key. That means little round pieces of carving. They slide or push or turn to open the panel. Trouble is, there are so many of them, everywhere you look. This whole place is wood-panelled to death!'

At that point they heard heavy footsteps beyond the door they had come in by. All three children froze. The footsteps stopped. Then the door was flung violently open with no thought to anyone who might be behind it.

'Marbles, Quentin,' Beans hissed, and Quentin dropped to the floor and joined the game. Beans tossed him a couple of marbles. One had a centre of yellow flame and the other a mix of scarlet and blue. From the corner of his eye he saw Scottie grab a book from the shelves and flop down on a window seat, as if utterly absorbed.

A pair of broad, perfectly shiny black toecaps appeared in view. Bent over his marbles, Quentin did a quick Holmes-type inventory. The smell of cigar smoke and lime cologne washed over the air. A man (sounding large, heavy-set) cleared his throat. 'Oh ho,' he said, in a distinctly unfunny voice, 'and what have we here?'

Beans looked up. Her face was a picture of small-girl innocence. 'We have marbles, sir. It's the perfect place for a game.'

'Not any longer, young lady. I shall be taking tea with Lady Sleete in here, and we do not wish to be disturbed. By marbles. Or children. Or indeed anything.'

Quentin took his scarlet-and-blue and aimed it at the marble nearest the invader's shoes, a solid tar-black globe, pitted and scarred from many battles. The black spun away and pocked loudly against the gentleman's right toecap. As if out of nowhere, a large hand shot down and grabbed it. The marble vanished inside his palm. His plump, jowly face had a smug expression on it and his eyes dared them to protest.

Beans sat back on her heels and glared at him. Quentin said, 'But—!' Scottie slid off his window seat and advanced towards them, the book held in his hand like a weapon.

At the far end of the room a footman swept in with a huge silver teapot, followed by a maid bearing a tray laden with cups and cake.

'Off you go, children,' the gentleman said, in an uncompromising tone. 'At once.'

'He took my Dark Star!' Beans cried, when they stood outside in the hallway again. 'My very best marble in the whole world. How could he?'

'That was Marmaduke Roxburgh,' Scottie told Quentin. 'He's supposed to be very important.'

'He's very *mean*,' growled Beans. '*And* rude. *And* pompous.'

'Important people are often pompous. They don't know how to be ordinary.'

'What is he important at?' asked Quentin.

Scottie put on his superior tone again. 'Oh, he's very rich and he invests in things. He's been asked here to meet Dad, or maybe Dad was asked here to meet him. Seems Lady Sleete is famous for getting rich and powerful and clever and interesting people together. Just to see what happens next.'

Quentin pictured his own parents. His father was in some dull kind of business, and spent a lot of time playing golf. His mother sat on charity committees and played a lot of bridge. Neither of them was rich or powerful. Or clever. Certainly not interesting.

'There's a well-known actress here, too,' Scottie was saying, 'and some kind of distinguished writer.'

Quentin didn't think that his parents were distinguished, either.

'How do you know all this?' he asked.

Scottie shrugged and walked away up the stairs. 'We keep our finger on the pulse,' he said.

'Don't take any notice of him. That's just one of Dad's phrases,' Beans said, nudging Quentin to follow. 'Honestly? Miss Kettle told us. She's a *mine of information*.'

'I'd like to meet her.'

'You will. It's teatime. She'll be waiting for us upstairs.'

'Did she warn you that Marmaduke Roxburgh was quite so beastly?'

'Um...no. But grown-ups never admit such things to children, do they?'

How true, thought Quentin; and he looked at Beans with new respect.

7 SERVANTS' HALL

NANCY'S JOURNAL

The ODDEST thing! I just bumped into someone I know.

Just on my way upstairs after tea in the Servants Hall & a boy was coming towards me. He was walking along & putting on a sweater at the same time—1 arm halfway thru a sleeve & his head still inside it so I couldn't see his face. I said 'Whoops—look out!' Probbly should have been more polite—but he nearly knocked me over. Then his head popped out the neck-hole & I said 'Quentin!' & he said 'Oh!' and then 'Nancy Parker!' and then 'Do you work here now?'

His name is Quentin Ives & I met him last summer at Seabourne. He's a funny kid—but not all bad for a Posh Boy who thinks a lot of himself. I asked what he was doing at Midwinter & he pulled a face & said his mum & dad were here for a visit. He's not seen them since he arrived & doesn't even know where their room was. (So I am not the only one confused.) I told him that I'm a Lady's Maid now & I was just here on a visit too. No need to go into Un-nesser-sary Detail.

Quentin said that some cousins of my old frend Ella Otter are staying here too. They have all been searching for Secret Passages—which is just like Quentin! His head is always full of daydreams about being a SPY and working undercover.

I suppose he could say my head is full of daydreams

too—of being a Detective—or an Actress someday. But at least I have solved a crime or 2 in my time. And if I keep practising my Acting—like Aunty Bee always says—'Who knows what may happen?'

Quentin told me his room is on the top floor (so is mine) & if we need to meet or send each other messages we should do it right here. Then he pointed to a funny old head carved into the bannister-post—some kind of Pirate or Soldier. Or someone with jaw-ache judging from the look on his face. (I don't know why Quentin thinks we may need to meet or send each other secret messages!! But he is a boy who loves Adventure & I dare say he is bored.)

At tea I met the other Visiting Servants. So far as I could make out there's

just one other ladies maid (the girl I'm sharing a room with) & a slimy-looking type that's Valet to someone called Sir Roxber. (Roxburr? Rocksbird?) There may be others to come—but it goes to show not everyone brings their own personal maid or manservant.

The other girl's name is ~~Sophy~~ Sophie Leblonk & she is French! (French ladies maids are said to be the best.) Not a girl really—more a young woman—v. pretty with dark hair & a cheeky smile. I expect her dress was French too for it had bags more style than my old frock even after Miss Bowman had spruced it up.

But the most exciting thing is that she is maid to Miss Lily Lopez—THE Lily Lopez!! So famous I've seen her picture in the papers. She starred in a show in London before Christmas & next week she begins rehearsals for a new play. Just hearing someone across the tea table from me saying those words—'begins rehearsals'—gave me a lovely shiver!

Wunder if I could get in Miss Lopez's good books? Maybe she will find a small part for me in her next play?? (I need another job after we finish here. Imagine going home & telling them that I'm off to work in a West End show!!) I wouldn't mind if I didn't have any lines to say. Better start by getting on the right side of Sophie Leblonk. Seems Miss Lopez has a bedroom down the hall from Miss Lamb's. I expect I shall see her soon!

All Lady Sleete's servants seem very OLD. They've been at Midwinter for years & years & I dare say the way they do things has not changed for years & years neither. It was a grumpy old housemaid who tapped on the Rose Room door & told me tea was waiting in the Servants Hall. Otherwise I would have been stuck here for ever with my stummick rumbling—not knowing what to do or where to go.

Another thing:- I wanted to write home but the Footman told me they were run off their feet & what with all the snow no one will be taking anything out to the post tonight. It's true you can hardly see out of the windows for snowflakes. But he sounded most un-obliging.

8 POOR MISS LAMB

NANCY'S JOURNAL

I like being a Ladies Maid! It's such A SOFT JOB compared with all the others I've done. No running back & forth every time a bell rings. No lugging great cans of hot water about or cleaning sooty fireplaces—yet always having to look neat & clean & <u>never</u> out of breath! When I was a general maid I scarce had a moment to sit down.

The only bit that's turned out <u>not quite so easy</u> is Miss Lamb. (I know every maidservant has to keep her Missus happy but usually that's simply about using the right brand of wax-polish or not spilling the gravy.) But poor Miss Lamb returned to the Rose Room most <u>adgitated</u> <u>& upset</u>. Not about straightforward things like gravy or polish neither. Seems that:-

* Lady Sleete in the flesh is an ABSOLUTE DRAGON & acted very nasty towards her.
* On arrival the ~~gets~~ guests had a grand tea in the Drawing Room & Lady Sleete only swept in when it was nearly done. Miss L. said 'Her cold manner from the start made it clear that she did not care for me. I beleeve she tried to trip me up with odd remarks & make me look a fool in front of the others. I was so nervous by then that I probbly <u>did</u> look a fool.'

41

* & the worst thing was that Dr James was not there to stick up for her!

Midwinter Manor may be hundreds of years old but they do have the Telephone installed. Dr James had rung to say he was stuck at the hospital & could not get away as soon as he planned. (Miss Lamb expected he'd be here when we arrived.)

Thinking to be helpful I said that of course he could not leave in the middle of sawing a leg off or something like that. But Miss L. said he was not that kind of doctor. He is an expert in Chests & Lungs & that's how she met him—during the War when he was treating her brother.

I had to calm her down so that she was in anything like a fit state to go to dinner. I tried to get her changed into an evening frock but she could not stop going to the window to peer at the snow. 'He will never get here!' she kept muttering. Then all of sudden she gave up pacing & flung herself into a chair. She said 'I didn't say this before, Nancy. BUT—'

Which made my heart sink. I've learned there's always something an employer—however nice they are—doesn't care to tell you BEFORE you take the job! Which to my mind is Trickery. And they all do it.

So this is what she didn't tell me at first:

Miss Lamb was not asked here just for a pleasant

New Year house-party where she'd meet her future Grandmother-In-Law. She is here to be INSPECTED as a Future Wife. Lady Sleete is to be Judge & Jury & decide if she is <u>suitable</u>. Miss Bowman knows all this. <u>That's</u> why her eyes stopped twinkling when the subjeck of Lady Sleete came up last night. (I knew something was up. See—my instinks were right!)

Yet how could such a nice lady as Miss Lamb NOT be suitable?? She's so kind & clever & was the best teacher at my old school.

This next bit sounds like a Fairy tale (tho a sad one): the Sleete family is very old & very fine but Lady Sleete had 4 children & all of them girls. Not one son to inherit the name. Those girls grew up & married & had children themselves. There were plenty of boys this time—3 of them older than Doctor James. But then the War came. Those boys went off to fight & didn't come back. That means James—who never expected it—will be the one to inherit Midwinter Manor & carry on the family line. So Lady Sleete is very bothered about who James will marry & 'she <u>does not approve</u> of his choice'. (Those were Miss Lamb's exact words.) That's becos Miss L. is just a lowly Schoolteacher & her father works in a Bank.

Well, where I live in Bread Street, being a Schoolteacher would be seen as a grand job—and working in a Bank even grander! I bet Miss Lamb's Dad wears a pin-striped suit &

a bowler hat to work every day. My Dad wears overalls &
every night they come back filthy.

Miss Lamb's dad

My Dad

Miss Lamb went on: 'To think that I teased James about
this visit. I thoght he was being uncharitable about his
grandmother—that she was just a little STIFF & STERN—
as old people can be. I was sure she would warm to me when
we met. But no!'

She looked v. downcast. It crossed my mind to say that
my Gran could be harsh but then I decided that was no
help. I do so wish Miss Bowman was here & it was not just

me having to do all the cheering up.

'James promised that he would be by my side,' Miss Lamb said. 'But now he won't get here for hours! And soon I have to go down to dinner and be <u>Bombarded with questions</u> again.'

To take her mind off things I changed the talk to the other guests & so I managed to get Miss Lamb into her frock & sitting in front of a mirror so that we could (between us) do something with her hair. That did <u>distract</u> her somewhat. She told me a funny story that Jasper Grant told about another famous writer who never eats anything but Tomato Soup! & then she discribed Lily Lopez for me in great detail. She is as beutiful up close as in the flattering newspaper pictures & seems frendly & not at all stuck-up. (Which is good news for me! I must try & get a word with her. Tho I can't give the game away about me & Miss Lamb. Hum ho—difficult—will think about this later.)

Then she said 'Nancy—if you are going to write all this down in your Journal you had better spell things properly. I know you of old!'

So it seems that if you want to say HEIR to the family fortune it isn't spelt the same as AIR. And 'fee-on-say' is really 'fiancé' with a little mark like a flame over the E. That French maid's name is written as Le Blanc—not Leblonk. And that Miss Bowman's name is really Beaumont (even tho she <u>isn't</u> French). That is the trouble with all these Frenchified words. They don't look like they sound. Not at all.

But at least Miss Lamb knows about my diary. I've always had to keep them secret before & steal time to write anything down.

Now she's gone downstairs—looking jolly handsome tho I say it myself! My job is just to wait about for her to come up to bed. So here I am sitting beside her fire writing this. My shoes are propped on the hearth & stuffed with newspaper—hope they will be dry by bedtime. All I can hear is the wind blowing yet more snow against the windowpanes. Now I just need something to read . . .

Cos that's what I forgot in all the rush to pack. Usually Aunty Bee passes on books from Lost Property at the Bus Depot where she works. You'd be supprised at the stuff people leave on buses—not just umbrellas & gloves—but cake boxes & false teeth & once a whole set of Fish Knives in a felt-lined box. If stuff isn't claimed it gets sold. But nobody wants to buy old torn copies of detective stories (Penny Dreadfuls my Gran calls them cos they used to cost just 1 penny) so Aunty Bee gets them for free. The more blood-spattered the cover the better we like them. The more puzzling the Crime is the better we like them too. I always bring some with me when I'm away from home—except this time.

I told Miss L. I forgot to bring a book & she said I

could try the Libary here. Mr Grant kindly showed it to her after tea. (I wunder if that's cos he spotted she was feeling all out of sorts?? The more I hear of Jasper Grant the more I like him.) She said she spied a few new books with bright paper covers. Not just <u>ainshunt tomes</u> so dry-as-dust that they would crumble if you opened them. 'You might like a Modern Novel, Nancy. They're not all worthy or dull. In fact' she added 'I may need some reading to take my mind off things if this visit is to be as horrid as I suspeckt!'

So that's what I'm waiting for—everyone to be busy eating their 2nd or 3rd course at dinner & drinking their 4th or 5th glass of wine—then I shall slip downstairs to the Libary. If anyone finds me I shall say I am fetching a book for Miss Lamb.

What a fancy bit of paper I pinched for this note!

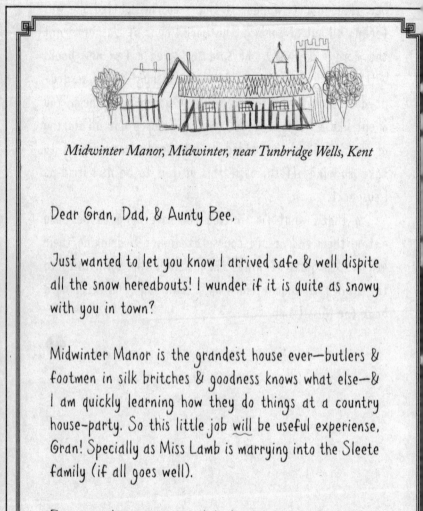

Midwinter Manor, Midwinter, near Tunbridge Wells, Kent

Dear Gran, Dad, & Aunty Bee,

Just wanted to let you know I arrived safe & well dispite all the snow hereabouts! I wunder if it is quite as snowy with you in town?

Midwinter Manor is the grandest house ever—butlers & footmen in silk britches & goodness knows what else—& I am quickly learning how they do things at a country house-party. So this little job will be useful experiense, Gran! Specially as Miss Lamb is marrying into the Sleete family (if all goes well).

But even better is that Lily Lopez—star of the West End stage!—is here. Not seen her yet. But I shall make sure I do. Plus there's a writer name of Jasper Grant

Midwinter Manor, Midwinter, near Tunbridge Wells, Kent

(have you heard of him Aunty Bee?) & someone called
Sir Marmaduke & even a Princess!! I am mixing in very
high-flown circles aren't I?

This house is tucked away in the countryside & I expect
it will be a quiet few days for me. My tasks as Lady's
Maid are a Piece of Cake!

All for now,
Nancy xxx

P.S. With the snow piled so high I am not sure how—or
when—this letter will reach you. I may be home before
you read this!

9 PREPARATIONS

Quentin heard an urgent tapping at his bedroom door; then a voice said, 'Quentin? It's Mummy. Have I got the right room?'

'Just—just a mo!'

In case she wouldn't wait just a mo, Quentin stuck out a foot to stop the door from opening. He looked around wildly. Preparations for exploring secret passages lay all about—torch, matches, extra thick socks, even a bit of charcoal from the fire to blacken his face. Hopping on his other foot, he swept them under the bed (thank goodness it was such a small room!) and grabbed his dressing gown. He was swathed in that and lying down with *The Christmas Annual for Boys* propped open before he called out, 'Come i-in!'

'It's very dark in here, Quentin. Are you sure you can see what you're reading, darling?'

Mrs Ives crossed the room and adjusted the shade on his bedside lamp. Bits of her evening dress glittered as she moved, and other bits of it jingled. When she bent over Quentin a strong waft of her perfume made him cough.

'Miss Kettle told me I'd find you up in the old nurseries,' his mother went on, surveying the room. 'I must say, it's terribly Spartan in here. Could do with lick of paint and a nice new carpet. Are you warm enough?'

Quentin nodded.

'Not too lonely?'

Quentin shook his head.

'I understand that you and Mr Otter's children have got to know each other already.'

Quentin nodded again.

'Do tell—what are they like?'

He faked a yawn. Best not to encourage his mother in any way.

But she sat down on his bed and rattled away. 'Lady Sleete has invited such interesting people. Mr Otter is perfectly fascinating. He's an American, you know, and a *millionaire*. How wonderful if you children became firm friends! I do want you to make a good impression, Quentin, and looking smart always helps.'

She clearly hasn't laid eyes on Scottie and Beans yet, Quentin thought.

Clasping her hands together in delight, Mrs Ives went on, 'I've chatted to a famous author and an adorable young actress. And an actual princess. Just think of that! Though she's extremely old and fearfully deaf. And then of course Sir Marmaduke Roxburgh—such a charming man!'

So charming he steals toys from children! But when it came to judging character, Quentin had learned that grown-ups were always easier to fool than children. Perhaps it was because children saw what was really going on, whereas grown-ups saw only what they wanted to see; though he would make an exception for the unique powers of Sherlock Holmes.

His mother wasn't budging. She trilled out a laugh. 'Really, your father and I must be the dreariest people here! We're quite without fame or fortune. I can't *think* why Lady Sleete invited us.'

Quentin knew that he was meant to respond with something flattering and reassuring. *Oh really, Mummy, what a silly you are! She invited you because of your wonderful...* But he had no idea, so he didn't say a word. Instead he let his book fall and yawned again, wider and louder. Then, to make the point, rubbed his fists into his eyes.

Mrs Ives watched fondly. 'You're tired, poor boy. What a long day you've had.'

'Mmm. G'night, Mummy,' Quentin mumbled, as if he could barely raise the energy to speak.

'Goodnight, dear.' His mother retreated to the door.

Quentin merely grunted. At last the door shut. He sat up and listened until his mother's footsteps faded into silence. Then he flung off the blankets and pulled on his extra socks.

***

'Ready?' said Beans.

Quentin nodded. He waved his torch. It was small, but in confined spaces, powerful; useful for reading under the covers and easily hidden beneath his pillow. 'I'm pretty good at investigating, if I say so myself. Had a bit of experience in the field, and more than a little success. The stories I could tell—'

Scottie interrupted. 'We'll start in my father's room,

with the panel we know about.'

Beans added, 'We're going to find out if there really is a passageway behind it.'

'Wait!' said Quentin. 'Sshh.'

They heard the sound of heavy feet just round the corner. One of the housemaids appeared, her arms full.

'Oh, hello, Pritchard,' Beans said in an over-cheerful tone.

Quentin stared at her. He couldn't tell one servant from another and he certainly didn't know any of their names.

Pritchard nodded at Beans. 'Still up, Miss? It's very late. Miss Kettle wanted me to see if you're cosy enough up here. I've brought hot water bottles. Snow's terrible tonight.' The housemaid trudged past and went into Scottie's room.

'We shall have to look as if we're on our way to bed,' Beans hissed.

The housemaid came out again.

Quentin improvised. 'I can lend you both some books. Nothing like reading to send you to sleep.' His voice sounded false, even to his own ears. Beans rolled her eyes. Quentin ran to fetch his new books and made a show of handing them over. 'Well, goodnight,' he said feebly. 'See you in the morning.'

The maid was in his own room now, arranging logs on the fire and taking her time about it. Servants really were the slowest, most dull-witted creatures . . . and then he remembered Nancy Parker. You couldn't say that of Nancy, not at all. She must be the exception to the rule.

10 CLAUSTROPHOBIA

It was not as he had imagined. Scottie began by twisting the middle of the carved Tudor rose and the thinnest crack appeared in the panelling. Then Beans pushed at the crack with the flat of both hands, carefully inching the panel open. An unimpressive space appeared. To Quentin it looked like the back of the toy cupboard at home when you reached inside for the box of dominoes or Snakes & Ladders. A secret passage ought to be grander than this, not just some almost *accidental* gap behind the woodwork.

Besides, wouldn't it be a perfect haven for mice and spiders? And what were those things that munched their way through ancient timbers? Deathwatch beetles—that was it! When you heard the knock-knock of deathwatch beetles in your walls you knew that time was up.

But Beans and Scottie were standing back, grinning proudly at him.

'You first,' said Scottie.

'No, honestly,' Quentin mumbled, 'you were the ones who found it.'

Beans shrugged. It was clear that she couldn't wait to

squeeze herself into this tiny, terrifying compartment. But Scottie, being older, elbowed her aside and ducked into the space. And disappeared! It scarcely seemed possible. Beans went next. After some moments of deep breathing, Quentin dipped his head, hunched his shoulders, and followed them.

First there was a narrow space behind the panelling, just wide enough and high enough to ease himself along. How on earth would a portly priest or a soldier wrapped in a winter cloak and carrying a sword ever fit themselves in here? Were people really so much smaller in the olden days?

His torch-beam shone ahead very brightly, picking out the back of Beans's head. The light made his eyes squint. Then her head vanished. There was a rapid right turn.

'Steps here,' Beans's whispered voice came back. The beam wavered over a sloping cobwebby roof and Quentin's foot suddenly whooshed from under him.

'Steps *down*,' Beans amended.

The steps were a little bit wider. Quentin no longer had to move sideways like a crab. Scottie had told him to leave his shoes in his room and come wearing two pairs of socks. 'Avoids making any sound,' he explained. Now Quentin could feel the thick wool of his outer socks catching on splinters in rough wood; it was like walking over a trap set with glue. And the ceiling with its hideous grey curtains of centuries-old cobwebs was so very close to his head. He pulled in his neck, squeezed in his elbows, and moved his feet with great care.

It was an adventure, but not the sort of adventure he actually enjoyed.

Scottie and Beans had come to a halt. Quentin was still on the stairs. He lowered his torch and could feel the darkness right behind him, black as a bat. The hairs on his neck prickled. What if a housemaid came into Mr Otter's bedroom to feed the fire and put a hot-water bottle in his bed? She might see the open panel and shut it. Then what?

He didn't think he had made a sound, but the two heads in front turned back to him and glared. Beans raised a finger to her lips. There was another sound, *beyond* the cramped passageway where they crouched. It came again.

Quentin leaned down as far as he could and whispered into Beans's ear, 'Coughing?'

Beans gave a single nod, then whispered back, 'Must be in the library. It's the only room on the ground floor of this wing.'

It was strange to crouch on the shadowy stairs, with his knees pressed into the back of a girl he barely knew, while up ahead a boy he barely knew lay his ear against a cobwebby wall and listened. While beyond, nearby, an unknown man coughed.

Quentin shifted his feet. One leg was getting cramp. Beans shoved her elbow backwards into his shin, urging him to keep still.

Then the sound changed. Voices were talking now. Deep voices. Male voices, definitely. It was impossible to make out the words, but the voices went on like gruff instruments playing a two-part tune. It wasn't a happy tune.

What if you had to hide like this for hours—for

days—Quentin thought, while the king's inquisitor, or the sheriff's men, or enemy troops, were just the other side of the wall?

A wave of heat rushed over him, followed by a wave of sickness. The thick socks were muffling his feet and legs unbearably, his sweater was engulfing him, the air all round him was soupy and foul. Did this mean that they were running out of oxygen? How long had they got left? Miners took canaries with them underground. When the bird keeled over, that was the sign to leave—in a hurry. They should have brought a canary! Quentin's neck prickled again, his whole scalp tingled. It felt like a thousand spiders running through his hair. It might actually be! He had to get out.

He poked Beans in the shoulder. 'Can't breathe,' he whispered, despite not being able to find any air in his lungs to whisper with.

She pulled a face.

'Foul air. Not safe,' he hissed. Beans just frowned and shook her head, as if he made no sense.

He backed up the stairs on his bottom, one step at a time. The torch joggled and the light zigzagged all over the crumbling walls and the grimy cobwebs. The banging of his heart inside his ribs would give them all away. It must sound like a massive bass drum. Then there were no more steps behind him. He couldn't see Beans or Scottie, only a dim glow from the torch Scottie held with his fingers over the glass.

Quentin stood up on wobbly legs, slithered around the turn in the passage, and eased his way back to the opening. He stuck his head out, not caring if the housemaid was there making the room comfy. But there was no one.

He staggered to a window and pushed back the curtains. The catch was stiff and even when it moved he felt something else pushing against the glass. But then it flew open, and icy air flew in. Quentin heard a heavy crump. He leaned out. The snow that had piled against the window now lay in a heap far below. It spoiled the flawless white blanket that covered the courtyard.

He hung out of the window and sucked in clean cold lungfuls. His fellow explorers were still in the tunnel, breathing foul air. Well, serve them right. Beans had refused to heed his warning. Quentin didn't like to think that they were made of stouter stuff than him. Especially as Beans was younger, and a girl. They were still in that cramped space, in the dark, with hordes of spiders. And probably deathwatch beetles! He shuddered all over again. He knew what it was: claustrophobia. His mother had it. That's why she wouldn't use the lifts at big hotels and department stores. They always had to go by the stairs. Quentin thought it was just one of Mummy's funny ways, but now he knew better.

He was beginning to freeze. Snowflakes landed on his cheeks and stuck in his eyelashes. He drew his head in and was about to pull the window shut when a movement caught his eye. A shape flitted across the courtyard from somewhere directly beneath him. Then it vanished into the whirling whiteness, gone so quickly that he wasn't even sure if he had seen anything at all.

11 THE BODY IN THE LIBRARY

NANCY'S JOURNAL

When I tripped over something on the Libary floor I wasn't expecting it to be

A BODY !

When I saw it <u>was</u> a body
—I didn't know it was DEAD !!

Not right away. I didn't even <u>scream</u>.

The only <u>dead body</u> I've ever seen before was old Mrs Parsons down our street. Gran insisted we go and pay our respects. There she was laid out in her coffin so neat & tidy & frozen-faced—could have been a waxwork for all I knew.

<u>This dead body</u> was different.

But I am getting ahead of myself. One step at a time. When it comes to writing about SUDDEN & MYSTERIOUS DEATH you must be scroop-u-lous about the details. (If you claim to be a detective. As I do.) (Even tho my fingers are starting to shake all over again just thinking about it!)

<u>What happened</u>: I waited long after the house went

quiet then followed Miss Lamb's instrucktions & found my way down to the Libary. She said I couldn't miss it—it's the only room on the ground floor in that wing. There was just one lamp lit & the fires at each end of the room had burnt down low. The books I wanted were on the shelves by the middle window. It was dim & shadowy so I didn't plan to hang about.

I took a quick look & chose 2 books—more like grabbed them—mostly cos of their pale covers. I was just turning round when my foot hit something.

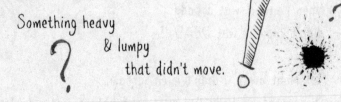

Something heavy
& lumpy
that didn't move.

I wundered if Lady Sleete had a dog that liked to sleep on floor of the Libary. But it was a VERY BIG DOG & it didn't grunt when I stepped on it—or growl at me—or indeed do anything.

I bent down to take a closer look & that's when I dropped my books. I may have let out a bit of a gasp. (I don't <u>think</u> it was a scream.)

What was lying slumped on the rug was A Man. I touched his shoulder—just to nudge him awake if he was sleeping. He DID NOT MOVE.

I could not smell Strong Drink—which may have caused

him to fall down like that. Only a whiff of Dr Banjay's Camphor Rub that Gran makes Aunty Bee put on her chest for that nasty cough of hers. (Working on the buses in the winter is <u>not</u> a cushy job.) His face was flushed dark. Like men In Drink <u>can</u> look.

One arm was flung out & the other lay on his chest reaching for his collar. Neither one of them MOVED. Not a twitch.

So I leaned nearer to see if I could hear breathing. NOTHING! So far as I could see his chest wasn't moving. His mouth hung open but he didn't gasp—or gurgle—or breathe at all.

I knew from all those crime books I've read that the next step is to <u>check for a pulse</u>. They never say <u>how</u>. The Doctor feels your rist—but what he is feeling for? I stared at the man's rists—the flung-out one & the one by his neck—but I couldn't bring myself to touch either.

But it was not the moment to be FAINT-HEARTED. I know I can be brave when it is called for. So I ran for the nearest door. It took me into a hallway—the one we came into when we first arrived. I reckernised that ugly great umbrella-stand full of wet black brollies. I shouted out something like 'Help! Help! A body! In the Libary!!!' If that didn't get people running nothing would.

A Footman appeared from one way & a lady who was coming down the stairs picked up her skirts & positively

<u>flew</u>. (This turned out to be Miss Kettle. As luck would have it she is the Practical Sort.) 'Fetch more lights!' she cried to to the Footman—which got him out the way. Then she let me drag her into the library. Her face when she saw that what I was shouting about was true!!

'Dear heavens!' she exclaimed & clutched at the neck of her dress. Rather like the poor Gentleman on the rug was doing.

The Footman came back—with several more fellows on his heels including the Butler—& several more lamps. Miss Kettle bent over the body & someone held a lamp close. Someone else insisted it was <u>not</u> A Job For A Lady! This was a large man with oiled hair & silver side-whiskers dressed in a v. smart evening suit. The pins in his snowy shirt-front glittered—I would hazard they were DIMONDS! He was quite determined <u>to be in charge</u>. He pushed in front of everyone & they got out of his way.

Miss Kettle said 'If only we had dear James to help us!' She meant Miss Lamb's fiancé.

'Isn't he here yet?' I asked. She shook her head. 'He promised to ring from Waterloo to say which train he was catching so Betts could drive out & meet him from the station—but we've heard no more. With so much snow I fear the trains have stopped. Oh & we are in such need of a Doctor here right now!'

Mr I-Am-In-Charge finished his ecksamination of the

body. 'Too late for a doctor I am afraid.' he announced. 'He's dead—but not yet cold.'

I think we all felt A Chill when he uttered those words!!

'Who is he?' he asked. Miss Kettle shook her head & said 'I've no idea, Sir Marmaduke. None at all. He is a Stranger.'

Sir Marmaduke looked round at all the shocked faces & wanted to know 'What is a stranger doing in Lady Sleete's library on a night like this?'

I wanted to add 'And what is he doing DEAD?'

Plan of where THE BODY was found (in case this may
Prove Useful.)

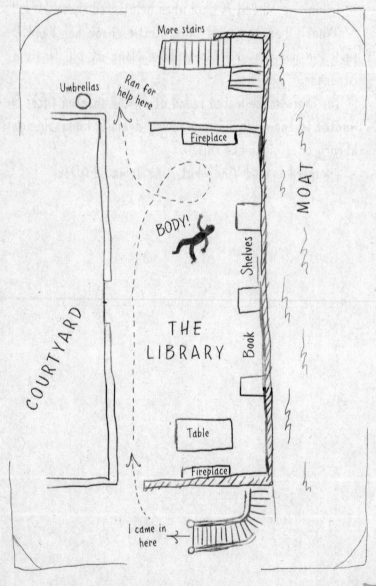

More stairs

Umbrellas

Ran for help here

Fireplace

MOAT

BODY!

Shelves

Book

THE
LIBRARY

COURTYARD

Table

Fireplace

I came in here

64

12 MISS KETTLE'S EYRIE

NANCY'S JOURNAL

Then Lady Sleete strode in. I knew it must be her. She had grey hair & jewels like you never saw & a long heavy dress of the old-fashioned sort favoured before the War. But it was her face that struck me. She was like a fearce great eagle I saw once at the Zoo—like she would EAT YOU FOR DINNER bones & all—then look around straight away for the next meal.

Sir (not Mr) I-Am-In-Charge said something about a Dreadful ~~Inser~~ Inssident. He tried to head her off as if she was bound to collapse in a Fainting Fit. But Lady Sleete is far from the collapsing type. For one thing her corsets won't let her! She came over & peered at the body thru her spectacles-on-a-stick.

Sir Marmaduke leaned over her shoulder & said 'Nobody knows who he is Your Ladyship'. (Tho I only heard him consult Miss Kettle.) 'An intruder. Very susspishus. We must summon the Police!'

Lady Sleete looked about at the other gents. There was a white-haired old man & a plump type with a large moustache—both in evening wear. She nodded to the Butler & he hurried out. (As far as any Butler DOES hurry—& this one is tubby as well.)

'Who found the body?' said Lady Sleete & her eagle eye went round again. I felt Miss Kettle's hand on my shoulder & my legs wobble under me. But just then the butler came rushing in saying that the telephone lines were down. Must be due to the snowstorm. So nobody can be summoned at present. Not Police or Doctor or any kind of help.

That's when all the gents started talking 2-to-the-dozen over each other & at Lady Sleete.

Miss Kettle patted my hand & said 'Come. You must sit down & recover from your DREADFUL SHOCK. Of course you will have to answer a few questions at some point. But they should come from someone in Or-thority.'

I grabbed my books which I'd dropped on the floor (didn't want anyone to wunder what they were doing there & not on the shelf where they belonged). I followed Miss Kettle out of the Libary & up the same stairs I came down in the first place. At the top she opened a door.

'Here's my little eye-rie' she said. 'Opposite Lady Sleete's rooms so that I can be on hand if she wants me. It is very peaceful. Please sit down. An eye-rie is the name for an eagle's nest, if you didn't know.' (And there was I thinking

Lady Sleete was the eagle!)

I was v. glad to sit. My legs felt WEAK & my heart was still thumping. I could see the poor dead gentleman as clear as day—even when I shut my eyes.

Miss Kettle remarked that I was better off here than in the Servants Hall where no doubt they'd press me to go over all the GRUESOME DETAILS. Which made me feel even more wobbly! I found the body. What if the Police think I was the One Who Did It??

Miss Kettle set about boiling water on the fire as if it was fine for her to be waiting on me. Then she went into the next room & came back with a small blue bottle. I thoght at first it was Smelling Salts but she poured a few drops into a glass of water & held it out to me. 'A little remedy for shock—I make it myself from herbs & such. It restores the Nerves. Lady Sleete swears by my remedies.'

I can't picture Lady Sleete ever being in need of such a thing. She looks like she has NERVES OF IRON.

I was still clutching my books. Miss Kettle kindly asked what I'd got there. I said they were for Miss Lamb & that's why I went into the Libary in the 1st place. 'She likes to read when she cannot sleep. And she finds it hard to sleep in a strange bed.' I knew I was babbling then so I shut up. I have no idea whether Miss Lamb is a sound sleeper or not. Tho whether any of us will sleep sound with a dead body in the house—& the telephone line down—& who knows how the body got there?—or how it ended up DEAD?

(I am babbling again—except on paper this time!)

Miss Kettle said 'I see you have one by dear Mr Grant.
He is such a favourite
of Lady Sleete.'
The cover looks
like this:

Snow &
Lilacs

Jasper Grant

Sounds a bit slushy to me. It may be a Romance. I don't
know if Miss Lamb reads that kind of thing. The other one
is 'Aunt Matilda Investigates' by someone called Coraline
Drake—that's more to my taste.

Next Miss Kettle made me a cup of strong tea & put
4 sugar-lumps in it. Strong sweet tea is good for shock.
(Tho at home Gran prefers a nip of brandy. For Medicinal
Purposes only.)

She said 'I must return to Lady Sleete now. I shall tell her what you told me. When you are recovered go along to your mistress's room. Miss Lamb and the other ladies were about to take coffee when this terrible thing ockurred. She will be upstairs soon & will be in need of you.'

So she left me alone beside the crackling fire. I could have stayed there <u>all night</u> to be truthful but after the tea & the Remedy I had to get moving. I slipped the books under my arm & something fluttered on to the hearthrug. A small card. I don't know if it fell out of Snow & Lilacs or if it came off the library floor when I snatched up the books. I have tucked it in here for safekeeping.

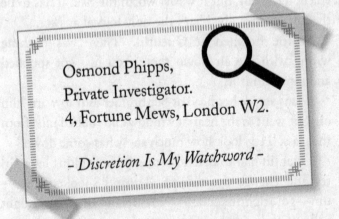

Osmond Phipps,
Private Investigator.
4, Fortune Mews, London W2.

- Discretion Is My Watchword -

I came straight back to Miss Lamb's room but as she is not here yet I've tried to put all this down AS A RECORD before I forget anything. Anything at all.

13 OLD HAT

Scottie and Beans emerged, breathless and tousled.

Quentin jumped up from the chair beside Mr Otter's writing table. 'Did you discover where the tunnel comes out?'

They shook their heads. Beans said, 'Didn't dare. We couldn't tell if there was anyone still in the room. The voices fell silent, but it wasn't worth the risk. It has to be the library, though. That's the only logical answer.'

Scottie frowned at Quentin. 'There was nothing wrong with the air down there. You just got spooked and ran. Admit it!'

Beans shook her head at her brother as if to warn him off. She went to the nearest window and rubbed mist from the glass. 'Hey, look how much snow has come down!'

Quentin had to defend himself. He couldn't let a girl try and change the subject. 'I *wasn't* spooked. Just—um—got frightful cramp in my leg and thought I might yell out and give the game away. It was safer for all of us if I cleared out.' Putting it like that made him feel quite noble. Even if it was claustrophobia rather than cramp, he had taken the right action. 'Are there any more secret passageways to explore?'

Scottie looked back at him with narrowed eyes, still suspicious. 'Sure you want to try again?'

Beans gabbled, 'Miss Kettle said there's loads to look out for. There's an ancient carved head on the stairs— have you seen it?'

'I might have…' Quentin said carefully.

'It's a Saracen. Something to do with the Sleete coat-of-arms. Then there are windowpanes scored with names and dates. Scratched into the glass with a diamond ring centuries ago! And family portraits with spaniels in them. The Sleetes liked to keep King Charles spaniels, because they were Royalists back in the Civil War.'

'Oh, come on, Sis,' said Scottie, 'you didn't know anything about the English Civil War until Miss Kettle told us about it. You didn't know there *was* one.'

Beans shrugged. 'I really like history.'

'I like more practical things,' Scottie declared. He gestured at some papers on the writing table. 'See those, Quentin. Dad's notes from his tour of foreign factories. There's valuable stuff in there. Dad gets his best ideas after talking to other people.'

Quentin thought it sounded as if Mr Otter *copied* other people's ideas, but he wasn't going to say so.

Scottie carried on, 'He sees what other people are doing wrong or could do better, and he listens to what they want to change but don't know how. Then he comes up with improvements, and sells them back to the people who couldn't come up with anything! I'd say that's a lot more useful than history.'

Beans yawned. 'I know inventing is useful . . . but not everyone wants to be an inventor. *I* don't. And history's useful too, if you learn from it.'

'History is *old hat*,' Scottie insisted. 'Fantastic new inventions are the stuff of the twentieth century. You'll see.'

Quentin found that yawning was catching. He covered his mouth and murmured, 'Time for bed, I think.' He would be glad to get away from Scottie, who reminded him of a know-it-all form captain at school. He still wasn't sure if his sister, with all her mad enthusiasm, was much better.

Beans beamed at him. 'We'll search for more secret passages in the morning!' she promised. Quentin stumped away with a heavy heart.

14 A HEAD FULL
OF QUESTIONS

NANCY'S JOURNAL

I am writing this in Miss Lamb's bathroom by the light of a single dim lamp!

Last night she came back to her room most adgitated. I heard her deep in talk with someone outside the door—too low to hear what was said. Turns out it was Lily Lopez (and I missed her!) Then Miss L. came in & asked me to sleep in her room instead of going upstairs. Tho how she thinks I can protect her from <u>a Murderer on the Loose</u> I don't know. Or how she can protect me! I didn't see her as the Nervous Type but none-the-less I was releeved. Still feeling shaky myself.

But the Rose Room couch is no good for sleeping on—not when you are tall & bony like me. Nor when you are <u>somewhat adgitated</u> yourself.

Plus my head is buzzing with QUESTIONS! The best way to sort them out is to write them down. First I must make a note of what Miss Lamb said happened at her end of the house—while it is still fresh.

What she told me:-

The ladies were taking after-dinner coffee when a Footman came in to drop a word in Lady Sleete's ear. She hurried away & everyone stared at each other—wundering what was going on. 'Mrs Ives thoght it was to do with the snowstorm but Miss Lopez felt it was something <u>much more exciting</u>.' Miss Lamb shook her head. 'To think that a stranger falling dead is exciting.'

I did say that they could not have known about the poor dead gent at the time & she nodded sadly.

Miss L. said that Mr Grant came in next & his usual jolly manner had changed to very ~~soulem~~ sollem. She <u>just knew</u> by this there was Grave News to come. She feared it was a train crash in the snow & that James was hurt. (Of course the ladies didn't know that the telephone wires were down so no news could get in. Or out.)

'But A CORPSE IN THE LIBARY!'—these were Miss Lamb's very words. 'We never expected that.'

No 'we' didn't. Not when we'd only gone in to borrow a book! But it wasn't the moment to tell her that. She was v. upset as it was.

Seems the ladies got into quite a flutter with Miss

Lopez declaring in her dramatic way 'Whatever next? Shall we be murdered in our beds?!' & Mrs Ives saying that at least she had Mr Ives to protect her. There was a Princess with them—a very old lady who kept nodding off—but she woke up at that asking 'Dead! Who's dead?' which set them all off again. At long last Miss Kettle came back, sent the cold coffee away & told them they must have Camomile Tea to soothe their nerves. (Which sounds just like her.)

So my questions are (trying to put them down in a Logical way even tho my mind is a-wirl):-

1. Is the dead man Osmond Phipps, Private Investigator?
2. Or was that card tucked in one of the books & just fell out by chance?
3. If he's not O. Phipps—WHO IS HE?
4. Why did no one reckernise him? Surely the servant who let him in would have spoken up?
5. So—who did let him in?
6. If nobody let him in—how did he get into the house?
7. He did not look like the sort who would break in thru a window. (A Ruffian or Burglar??) Besides he had to get over the moat to do that.
8. WHAT DID HE DIE OF?
9. No sign of blood or bullet wounds or a blow from a blunt instrument—but I could not make a detailed ecksamination.

75

10. Or poison. Would that be harder to tell at 1st glance?
11. Or was it Natural Causes?? (He was not a young man, I could see that much.)
12. If it wasn't Natural Causes—someone must have done it. WHO???
13. Is that someone still in the house?!
14. And here's a horrible thing—he was still warm. Or at least not cold. That means he was NOT LONG DEAD.
15. So whoever did it would be NOT LONG GONE!!
16. I might have run into him (or her?!) if I'd gone in there few minutes earlier.

I have some experiense solving criminal matters—but nothing as grave as MURDER!

15 HAVEN'T SLEPT A WINK

NANCY'S JOURNAL

I expected to find the Servants Hall <u>seething with gossip</u> at breakfast. But it was very quiet. Long faces all round & the manor house servants in a rush to get on with their work—as if they had been <u>ordered to keep their mouths shut</u>. (Well—a dead body on the libary floor is a HUGE SCANDAL.)

When I sat down Sophie Leblonk whispered that she was supprised to find me ALIVE & WELL this morning. Then she gave a sly wink! Of course—my bed had not been slept in. I whispered that Miss Lamb was too worried to be on her own last night. I dare say I looked like Death Warmed Up. (That's what Gran says when she's had a bad night with her roo-matticks.) Yet next to me Sophie appeared in v. good spirits & as pretty as a posy. Must have slept well dispite all the panic. Added to which I wasn't there to disturb her.

I was glad to get out of there soon as I could. I left Sophie at the table alone with Sir Marmaduke's toffee-nosed valet. When I looked back they had their heads together—seemed to have found something urgent to chat about. (Perhaps it was <u>me</u>!)

Next I took Miss Lamb a nice pot of tea. She sat up in bed & said 'What a dreadful night! I don't think I closed my eyes once.'

Now I know from sharing the back bedroom at Bread

Street with my Aunty Bee that when people claim 'they haven't slept a wink': well, they have. Cos you can hear the kind of slow breathing that goes with proper sleep. Even a bit of snoring from time to time. It's just that they <u>think</u> they haven't shut their eyes at all. When I got up in the middle of the night Miss Lamb was sleeping like a baby. (She wasn't the one who <u>stepped on a corpse</u>!!)

She asked if I knew whether Dr James was here yet & when I shook my head she twisted her hands together saying 'I <u>do</u> wish he would hurry up.' She hasn't seen how deep the snow is this morning!

I tried to help Miss L. get dressed but we kept tripping over each other. In the end I just handed her things when she asked for them. We managed to make quite ordinary chitchat about Clothes & the Weather—& take our minds off things like <u>corpses</u>—when we were inter-rupted by a knock at the door. A maid come asking for me! She said I was to go along to Lady Sleete's apartments as soon as Miss Lamb could spare me. I knew from her face that Lady S. expected Miss Lamb to spare me <u>right away</u>.

'It's about you finding the body,' she went on.

'Finding the body?!' cried Miss Lamb. 'Oh Nancy! You didn't?'

She looked so HORRORFIED that I felt I really shouldn't leave her just then. But the maid was keeping the door open so all I could say was 'Sorry, miss. Yes I did.'

16 A STRANGE SILENCE

Quentin opened his eyes. Something was very strange. He sat up in bed. The house was silent, which was odd. It was such an old place and sounds travelled: footsteps, muffled voices, floorboards creaking. Now—nothing. And it was *very* cold. All that was left of last night's fire was a heap of ashes.

He swung his feet out of bed and pushed them into his slippers. Wrapping himself in his dressing gown, he shuffled across the room and pulled one curtain back from the windowpane. There was nothing there. Correction, there was a thick whitish wall of something, something that entirely blocked his view of the outside world. He put one hand to the glass and felt the freezing air coming off it. Snow!

But—snow to the very top floor windows?!

'Scottie? Beans?' he called out, dashing into the corridor.

Scottie's door was shut. He tapped; no answer. So he opened it. The room was empty, the fire long-dead. Beans's room was empty too, and just as cold.

Quentin began to feel seriously worried. Midwinter Manor was buried to the rafters in snow and it seemed that everyone had fled. Except, if it *was* buried in snow, how did they get out? Perhaps there was another secret passageway, underneath the moat, that everyone knew about—and they had escaped that way. And forgotten all about *him!* Even his parents had forgotten! Unless they, too, lay in bed, quite unaware of what had happened overnight. If only he knew where on earth their bedroom was, on what floor, in which wing . . . This house was really preposterous.

By the time all these thoughts had flown through his brain Quentin was at the top of the staircase and clutching the fierce carved head with his right hand, his knuckles turning white. Had he really been abandoned?

Then his fingers found something there, something that wasn't ancient wood or slippery varnish: something crisp, but that bent with his touch. A piece of paper, folded small and tucked between the man's wooden hat and the bannister-post. A note!

This was the exact place he had suggested for secret communications between himself and Nancy Parker. Perhaps she'd tried to tell him what had happened to the rest of the household. He picked at the folds until the note came open.

Dear Q.

In case they keep it from The Children—this is to inform you there has been A MURDER! What's more—I was the one that found THE BODY. Must meet. Cannot tell when I will be free to speak to you so try to check this place every hour. Will do my best to get here soon as I can.

N.P.

Quentin stuffed the note into his dressing gown pocket. He could hear his own heart thumping in his ears. Could it be true? That someone was dead—murdered— who!? Was that why everyone had disappeared? But if that was the reason, where had they gone and what were they up to? Especially when it looked as if Midwinter Manor was entirely cut off by the snow. That meant that the murderer was still about. And if *that* was the case, why had they left Quentin all alone?

17 MISS LAMB AND MISS LOPEZ

While he stood there, dumbfounded, a housemaid came up the stairs towards him; she had a worried look on her face. I'm not surprised, Quentin thought. Dead bodies all over the place, and snow as high as the top floor.

'Oh, Master Ives, there you are! I was sent to fetch you. No nursery breakfast today. Everything's served downstairs, to save the bother. Hurry, if you please, before it's all gone.'

She trotted off, not seeming to notice that he was still in his dressing gown. Quentin followed. The lower floors were still unnaturally quiet, as if everyone was creeping about on tiptoe.

Breakfast was laid out in a large, cold room, panelled in dark wood, and hung about with pieces of ancient armour: breastplates, helmets, and swords. The window-panes were plastered with snow, but through the gaps he could see a snow-covered courtyard. The drifts were high, but not up to the rooftops. How could he have thought that?

Below the windows was a long table with only two

people seated at it: youngish ladies, one dark and one fair. The dark-haired one looked up when he came in and smiled at him, the other went on spreading butter on her toast.

Was this what people did when there had been a murder in the house, Quentin wondered? Just carry on as if nothing had happened?

'Help-yourself is the order of the day,' said the one who was buttering toast. 'We are late risers, but you're even later. Not a lot left, I'm afraid.'

'I'm sure you could ask for more toast,' said the other lady. 'My name is Araminta Lamb, by the way.'

'How d'y'do,' Quentin mumbled, not sure if he should shake hands. Her hands seemed to be full of teacup anyway. His mumble sunk lower, into a kind of growl. 'I'm Quentin Ives.' He hated that name. How much better it would be if he could say *Sherlock Holmes* instead. *Holmes of Baker Street . . . you may have heard of me.*

Araminta Lamb, though. Another awkward name. It summoned up roast lamb and mint sauce. Suddenly his stomach squawked, reminding him how starving he was. The last time he'd eaten was yesterday at nursery tea with Miss Kettle and the Otter children. Just dainty sandwiches and fairy cakes, nothing more substantial. He was a growing boy.

The fair-haired lady was watching him with a teasing smile. She propped her chin on one hand, and that hand had blood-red nails!

'Hello there, Quentin. I'm Lily Lopez. I believe I had the pleasure of meeting your ma and pa last night. They were down here earlier. You've just missed them.'

It came to Quentin, rather late, that at least the dead body wasn't either of his parents. *That* possibility had never crossed his mind. Which was a pretty strange thing to be thinking while your stomach was doing cartwheels to get your attention. Nothing for it, hunger must come first.

The sideboard bore an imposing set of heated dishes with silver covers, promising a good breakfast, whatever Miss Lopez said. He began lifting lids and peering underneath. What he found was a greying splotch of porridge, the last two rashers of bacon, an extremely small sausage, a single hard-boiled egg. Four more dishes were empty and one smelt strongly of kipper. Quentin seized a plate and spooned everything on to it. The hard-boiled egg he slipped into his pocket for later. Clearly, you had to plan ahead in this place.

He sat down at the table, keeping his distance from the ladies. The one called Lily Lopez had a larger-than-life face, with luminous blue eyes and perfectly even features. Even in the cold white light of the snow she looked like peaches-and-cream. Lamb-and-Mint-Sauce was a very ordinary sort of mortal beside her. They put their heads together, whispering, which Quentin thought was pretty rude of them. He concentrated on trying to spread cold hard butter on a crumbling bread roll.

Miss Lamb cleared her throat. 'Um, Quentin—I don't suppose you've spoken to your parents this morning, have you?'

Quentin shook his head.

'It may not be my place to tell you, but we—Miss Lopez and I—think you should hear this sooner rather than later. It would be unfortunate if it fell to the other children to say—'

Quentin interrupted. 'D'you mean about the murder?'

Their faces were a picture. Miss Lopez covered her mouth with a dainty hand and Miss Lamb looked as if she had swallowed a kipper, bones and all. 'There hasn't been *a murder*, Quentin,' she said gently. 'More of an accident.'

'*In*cident, I think, to be honest,' Miss Lopez said. 'We don't know for sure.'

Quentin watched them exchange secretive glances.

'The dead body, then?' he tried.

Miss Lamb waffled, 'Well. Yes. Sadly someone has—er—passed away. We've been discussing it. Apparently a gentleman who came to see Lady Sleete on some estate business was taken, um—'

'Taken ill, it appears,' Miss Lopez helped her out.

'And then dropped dead,' added Quentin. 'On estate business . . . A farmer, or tenant, or something?'

'Certainly no one to do with the house party,' Miss Lamb hurried on. 'You mustn't worry. It's just rather horrid and sad. We're trying not to dwell on it. Nor must you, Quentin.'

'Looks as if you've dwelt on it already,' Miss Lopez said dryly. 'At some length.'

'Lily!' said Miss Lamb.

Miss Lopez shrugged. 'We all have, darling. It's only natural. Unexplained dead bodies have that effect.'

Miss Lamb looked at Quentin, her brown eyes wide with sympathy. 'How *did* you find out?'

'From one of the servants, actually.' It was quite true; and should keep them happy, as long as he didn't say who, or how.

'Oh, dear. I suppose they couldn't help blurting it out. They're all at sixes and sevens today.'

Again Miss Lamb glanced at Miss Lopez for help. But Miss Lopez shrugged, raised her perfectly arched eyebrows and said, 'I'm absolutely gasping for coffee. Under the circumstances tea simply won't do. Where's that blasted footman got to?'

Quentin put his head down and attacked the last bits of sausage and bacon. His stomach gurgled thanks.

18 AS GUILTY
AS A MURDERER

NANCY'S JOURNAL

Lady Sleete's rooms are the grandest I've ever seen—if a bit old & crumbly. All frayed silk sofas & gold-framed paintings & giant ~~taper~~ tappestries with holes in. There was even a sofa for a <u>dog</u>. A little dog that put its chin on its paws & watched me without blinking as if it knew just what was being said.

Becos they called me there to be IN-TERROR-GATED!

Lady Sleete eagle-eyed me thru her spectacles-on-a-stick but scarcely said a word. Just kept sucking on lozinges from a little tin & glaring. It was the white-haired gent from last night who did the talking. He's the Sleete family lawyer & his name is Hawk. (Which suits him.) He may be old with a crooked back but he's still very sharp & fearsome. I didn't know which one of them was going to be first to pounce on me & gobble me up!

If only I'd had the chance to smooth my hair or press my frock. And after such a bad night as well. I know I looked a Fright. But that's when the Acting Skills came in handy. Told myself: pretend you're the <u>Star Witness</u> at an important trial. You didn't kill anyone—you just found the body. Chin up. Look them in the eye & tell them the whole truth & nothing but the truth.

(Except for the bits I aimed to keep to myself.)

But I must have looked AS GUILTY AS A MURDERER. Cos that's how they made me feel.

MR HAWK'S QUESTIONS
(HOPE I'VE REMEMBERED THEM ALL) :-

* What was I doing in the library?
* Was anyone else with me?
* When did I go in there?
* How long was I in there?
* What did I <u>see</u>?
* What did I <u>hear</u>?
* How did I come across the body?
* Was he already dead?
* How could I tell?
* What did I do next?
* <u>Why</u> was it Miss Kettle I told?
* <u>When</u> did I tell Miss Kettle?
* Did I tell anyone else?
* Did I know who he (the body) was?

I replied as clear as I could—in particular the bit about 'was he already dead?'

I didn't say that I was there to borrow books for myself—nor that Miss Lamb told me to wait til everyone was out the way. How I put it (quite clever really) was that I chose to go when I would not be disturbing anybody.

Of course I did not menshun I told Quentin Ives all about it in a note!! (Hope he had the sense to DESTROY it.)

And I did not say anything to the last question. Just shook my head.

I'm keeping my Theory about the Private Investigator to myself. Becos you never know—it DOES NOT ALWAYS PAY to be truthful with Those In Charge! They can turn on you. I've found that out—to my cost—before.

(Good thing that this Journal is in a v. small notebook that I can keep on my person at all times!!)

Me being in-terror-gated

Blushing cheeks

Guilty look

Sweaty hands

Hidden notebook

NOT how a ladies maid's dress should be:

19 ACCUSED

It was two minutes before eleven. Quentin hurried up to the top floor, hoping that Nancy would be waiting. But what he saw there wasn't Nancy, in dull black, but Beans and Scottie Otter in their garish sweaters. They swung round the bannister-post as they started down the stairs. Scottie's hand was actually *on* the Saracen's head.

'Quentin!' Beans halted, looking surprised; possibly even embarrassed. Well, it *had* been jolly mean of them to go off to breakfast without telling him. Without even waking him. Leaving him to imagine some frightful disaster had befallen Midwinter Manor. Indeed, it had; just not the one he'd imagined.

'Ah, Quentin,' said Scottie. He looked down with a sort of menacing casualness Quentin was familiar with from school. Bullies acted like that when they knew they had the upper hand.

'Terrible news, Quentin,' Beans gasped.

Quentin tried to look as casual as Scottie. He stuck one hand in his dressing gown pocket and stared into space in a kind of Sherlock Holmes lost-in-thought manner. 'I know. Terrible. A dead body in our midst. What in heaven's going on here?'

Beans turned red under her freckles. She glanced back at Scottie, who nodded his head as if to say, 'I'll handle this.'

'That's not all,' he said. 'Some important papers have gone missing. They were found to be missing this morning. Important papers belonging to our father.'

Quentin felt relieved. There was nothing he could do about that, and it was nowhere near as nasty as a dead body lying about the house. An *unexplained* dead body. He craned to see if Nancy was lurking about. But he couldn't meet her with the Otter children nearby. He hadn't told them about Nancy, and now that they'd turned all strange and threatening (well, only Scottie, but even so) he was glad he hadn't mentioned her.

'The thing *is*,' Beans began, 'the thing *is*, Quentin, that the papers disappeared from Dad's room. From a box on his writing table, to be exact. They were there yesterday, and today—this morning—they've gone.'

Scottie and Beans both stared at him, exactly as if they expected him to provide the answer. He may have suggested last night that he had some experience in solving crimes and even in catching criminals, but how he was supposed to come up with the solution to this? They'd only just informed him, and given him no more than the barest details to work with.

'These were vital papers,' Scottie said. 'You know our father invents things. He's been working on something new and had just about got it all down in his notes. Then they vanished.'

'My goodness!' Quentin tried to sound more affected than he actually felt. The Otter children were clearly proud of their father's achievements and very struck by the loss of these papers. 'I'm sure they'll turn up soon. Probably a housemaid has moved them. Not knowing how important they are. Or—or . . .' He couldn't come up with any more ideas.

'The crucial point, Quentin,' Beans said firmly, 'is that *you* were in our father's room last night. Weren't you?'

'Yes! *But,*' Quentin spluttered, 'I was in your father's room, with the pair of *you*, to explore the secret passageway that *you* were mad keen to show me! I would never have gone there otherwise. I didn't even know where your father's room *was*.'

Beans went on, 'But you came out of the passageway long before we did. You had at least five minutes—'

Scottie interrupted. 'At least *ten*.'

'—As much as ten minutes before we followed you out. And where did we find you?'

'I was hanging my head out of the window. I needed fresh air.'

'No,' said Scottie. 'No—you were sitting at Dad's writing table. *That's* where you were.'

Oh cripes! thought Quentin. So I was. I didn't want to look like a gasping wheezing panicky baby, so I quickly sat down at the table and pretended that I felt perfectly calm.

'We haven't told Dad it was you,' said Beans. 'Not yet. But we will, if you don't—'

'If I don't *what*?' asked Quentin. Solve their problem? He wished now he'd never claimed any likeness to Sherlock Holmes whatsoever.

Scottie hovered over him like a thundercloud. 'We're giving you a chance. Just this one chance. To hand those papers back, right now.'

'But I—'

'If you don't, we're going to tell Dad.'

'I can't hand back something I haven't got.'

Scottie just looked at him in scornful disbelief.

20 SECRET MEETING

Quentin fled back to his bedroom. It was bitterly cold. No one had been in to tidy or rebuild the fire. Snow still coated the entire window, making the room feel like a prison. He couldn't work the catch to open it and scrape off the snow; it was stuck, frozen shut.

Quentin sat on his unmade bed and tried to think. He was stunned, as if someone had actually punched him in the head. Why on earth would the Otter children think he was the thief? He hadn't a clue about Mr Otter's work and wouldn't know how to spot notes about an amazing invention unless they were headed *Amazing New Invention! Top Secret! Do Not Read—Let Alone Steal!!* They'd be accusing him of the murder next.

At that grim thought, Quentin shivered from head to toe. He jumped up and dressed in as many clothes as he could fit on over his pyjamas. His thick dressing gown went back on top. He dragged the front panels together and tied the cord tight. The world had gone mad, and he didn't care if he looked like a madman. At least he wasn't freezing any more.

He would find his parents and make them take him home. At once. He loathed Midwinter Manor. So must they. Surely they didn't want to stay here with a murderer on the rampage? And where their son had been accused of theft? Mummy would throw her arms around him and Father would roar with fury when he heard. Quentin ignored the fact that the snow was probably too deep for any vehicle to get through. Or that his father would never put his brand-new car at risk. They must leave. There was no other choice. He still had no idea of where his parents' bedroom was or where they might be in the house. But he had to find them.

Flying round a corner, he crashed into someone.

'Oof!' Nancy Parker took a step backwards. 'Quentin! I was coming to look for you.'

'Sorry, Nancy. I *did* try to meet you on the hour, as promised. But I'm in a fearful hurry now.'

'In a hurry off to beddy-byes?'

Quentin stuck his hands in his dressing gown pockets, pulling it straight. 'No, actually. Off to find my parents. They're going to take me home.'

'Got a magic wand, have they? Or a flying carpet?'

Quentin thought her sarcasm was quite unnecessary. 'I can't bear another minute in this place. It's just too awful.'

Somewhere nearby footsteps creaked over a wooden floor. Nancy slid into the shadows by the stairwell and peered inside a narrow door. 'This'll do. Quick!' She dragged Quentin with her. They were in a cupboard, with barely enough light to see each other's faces. Quentin stepped on something: a broom. He moved away and clanked against a dustpan.

'Sshh!' Nancy sounded impatient. 'I thought you *wanted* adventures? You were the one going on about secret messages and secret meetings.'

'Listen,' Quentin hissed back. 'Cosway Otter's lost some secret papers and his children think *I* took them! They were friendly enough last night when we went exploring, but now they've turned against me.'

Nancy shook her head. 'Think that's bad? *I've* just been interrogated about finding that body in the library.'

'What!' said Quentin and then, as her words sunk in, 'Where?'

'Where what?'

'Where did you say the body was found?'

'The library.'

'That's where the secret passage leads to! Or where Beans and Scottie think it leads to. We couldn't prove it last night because we heard voices.'

'What d'you mean, you heard voices?'

'We didn't dare go too far down it—because there were voices on the other side of the wall!'

'Of course there were voices!' said Nancy. 'Cos once I raised the alarm loads of people came rushing in, asking questions and giving orders all at the same time. That's who you heard.'

Quentin shifted his feet again and the broom-handle fell against his back. 'Must we hide in here? I'm not awfully keen on confined spaces.'

'You don't want anyone to see us whispering together, do you? They might think you're in league with a maidservant over those stolen papers.'

If this was Nancy's idea of a joke it wasn't funny. Nor was being shut in this horrible cupboard. He badly needed fresh air. But something urgent was trying to worm its way to the front of his brain. The *voices!*

'It wasn't a whole crowd of people that we heard. Just two men talking. One of them had a cough.'

'What did they say?'

'I couldn't make out actual words.'

'What time was this?'

'We waited until the grown-ups had gone to dinner.'

Nancy grabbed Quentin's arms and danced a little jig in the cupboard. There wasn't room, but somehow she managed it.

'Know what you've done?'

Quentin shook his head, wishing she would let go.

'You've found a valuable clue—evidence—something . . . You've made a key discovery in the investigation!'

'But what about the stolen papers?'

Nancy's eyes narrowed. 'A murder *and* a theft. Could be a connection . . . '

Quentin said, 'Do they honestly think that you're involved? In the murder, I mean?'

'I was scared they did. But I wouldn't be here now if that was the case. Lady Sleete and Lawyer Hawk would have me clapped in irons and dragged away. No—they were more interested in knowing if I heard or saw anyone *in the vicinity!*'

'And did you?'

'Sounds like *you* heard more than me. But don't tell anyone else yet. Might not be safe. Not until we know more.'

'Not safe?' Quentin definitely needed air now. 'Must go—get out—breathe.'

He opened the cupboard door and stumbled outside.

As he went Nancy said, 'Oh, if you want to find your mum and dad, try the Red Room in the North Range.'

'The North Range? Which one is that?'

Nancy rolled her eyes. '*This* one.'

21 REAL & HERE & NOW

NANCY'S JOURNAL

Poor old Quentin. He has his good points—leastways I think he does. I know he can be brave when he tries. He got my Journal back for me last summer when it was lost. Went into the JAWS OF DANGER to do it. But today—instead of worrying about The Murder—he's in a right old tizzy over being blamed for some missing papers.

Thing is, it's easy to suspeckt the wrong person—or any number of people—when you are trying to solve A Mystery. Like Lady Sleete & Mr Hawk thinking it was SUSPISHUS that I found the body. When anyone can trip over a body in the gloom—if a body is there to be tripped over in the 1st place.

Then sometimes you go for the wrong person becos the criminal deliberately makes it look like someone else's fault. That is called INCRIMINATING someone.

So now we have 2 crimes at Midwinter Manor in just one night.

1. A gentleman was murdered in the libary.
2. Somebody stole important papers from Mr Cosway Otter.

But—

3. The snow is so deep—& it is still snowing—that nobody

has got in or out of the house overnight.

4. So the Theef & the Murderer must still be here.
Perhaps they are one & the same.

5. The telephone lines are down so nobody outside
Midwinter Manor knows about these crimes—

6. —or is coming to help!

Now I have written it down like that A CHILL has gone
up my spine. Nothing to do with the wintry weather.
Everything just looks so sinister & scary put down in
black-&-white. This isn't some lurid crime story that I'm
reading to wile away the time between my tasks.

IT'S REAL
& HERE
& NOW

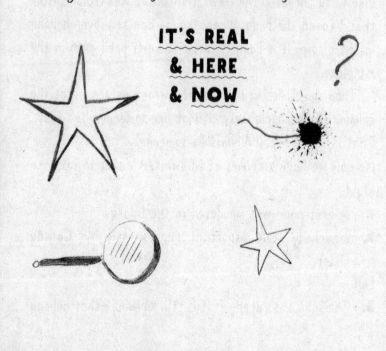

22 ONE LADY'S MAID TO ANOTHER

NANCY'S JOURNAL

I was sitting on my bed writing all that down when Sophie Leblonk came into our room—which is why I had to stop all of a sudden. (I know that according to Miss Lamb I should spell it Le Blanc but to me that just doesn't look right. No one but me is reading this—so I shall spell it how I please.) Hid this book in the folds of my skirt—stuck my hands over it—& tried to look THE PICTURE OF INNOCENCE. Too late!

'What are those papers? Show me! Are you reading or writing something?' Sophie has a playful way about her—but I could tell she meant to find out & would not stop til she did.

Lucky for me I remembered something just in time—an old book about Household Management from my last job full of tips on How Things Should Be Done. The author (a bossy old baggage called Lady Pouncey) said lists must be kept of everything. Like who comes to visit & what food is served so the same menu is not offered twice. Even what outfits the Lady of the House wears so it doesn't look like she's only got 1 good frock. So I made out I was keeping a notebook for Miss Lamb—what clothes & jewels she wore each day. (As if she has heaps to choose from!!)

Sophie exclaimed 'That is so clev-AIR!' Which is how she speaks, being French. 'So help-FOOL I must also do that for Miss Lo-PEZ.'

She wanted to see exactly what I was trying to hide. We had a bit of a tussle but I'm taller & my arms are longer than hers. She had to give up trying to grab the notebook from me & sat on her own bed laughing till the tears ran. (Is that how the French usually behave?) Clapped her hands & kicked her heels so hard against her suitcase that it disappeared right under the bed. Almost as if she had something there she didn't want me to see.

'Don't wor-REE. I av no wish to read your private notes' she said. 'What if you put something bad about me? Or Miss Lopez?'

'Why would I do that?' I replied. (Sometimes it's easier to ask a question so you don't have to tell a lie!!)

We got talking about all the lovely clothes & jewels Miss Lopez has with her. Sophie promised to show them to me when there is a quiet moment. (Tho it is Miss Lopez herself I would rather see. I want to meet the Actress—not the frocks.) But Sophie spoke like one Lady's Maid to another so I must be convincing. Phew!!

I fear she is a mind-reader tho! Her very next words were that Lily Lopez is far better at being a CLOTHES-HORSE than an Actress. The top fashun houses lend her dresses to wear cos she's a walking advertising poster.

Every hostess wants her at their parties & Lords & Dukes & whatnot like to be seen with her on their arm. They even give her jewels! I asked if Lily was engaged. Sophie said 'No. But if she cares to marry she can take her pick. She casts her spell over everyone & they fall at her feet.'

I started to leave but Sophie grabbed my hand & told me she had heard some gossip about _me_. She wanted to know all about finding the dead body. (Miss Kettle said the servants would grill me for gruesome details.) I said was I was NOT AT LIBERTY to speak in the hope that would shut Sophie up.

She is a most insistent girl.

That's why I came down here to Miss Lamb's bedroom. Much more Private.

I'm coming to think that Sophie is rather 2-faced. Half the time she sounds annoyed—almost jellous—when she's talking about Lily. You'd think a proper French Lady's Maid would adore having a Clothes-Horse for a mistress & enjoy every bit of sucksess she had. Also I noticed that when she's angry Sophie sounds less & less French in her way of speaking. Most odd.

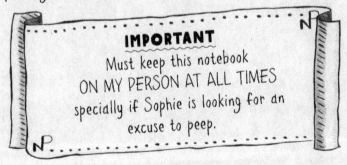

IMPORTANT
Must keep this notebook
ON MY PERSON AT ALL TIMES
specially if Sophie is looking for an
excuse to peep.

A scribbled note—in case you get back here before I do, Nancy. Lily has just put her head round the door and we are going down to breakfast together shortly.

I must apologize for going on and on about my worries without giving anyone else a thought. How shocking for you to be the one to discover the poor deceased gentleman!

I expect Lady Sleete simply wants to hear your side of the story. If you need my help in any way, of course you can count on it, and as soon as James gets here he will be able to vouch for you.

On a completely different matter, I wish to wear my green silk blouse later, but it is terribly creased. Please could you arrange to have it pressed.

Thank you.

Araminta Lamb

23 OVERHEARD

NANCY'S JOURNAL

Miss Lamb left that note in The Rose Room—pinned to her nightgown so I would see it when I tidied up. (Didn't spot it at first. I was so busy writing my notes!) Does she really think I will <u>need her help</u>? How can Dr James vouch for me? We've never met. Why do I need anyone vouching for me??

Hand on heart—I think I did a pretty good job <u>speaking up for myself</u>.

Just scribbling this in the Ironing Room. (They have a whole room for it!) I nipped downstairs to find someone to press Miss L.'s blouse—seemed like a GOOD EXCUSE to get among the Midwinter servants. I've discovered the trouble with being a Lady's Maid is that you are not <u>right in the middle of things</u>. You can't just walk into a room with a tea tray or a dustpan like you are meant to be there. You are far below Them Upstairs—but Them Downstairs don't like you neither. Which means you miss hearing & seeing so much that may be useful. Specially when you are really a Detective In Dissgize.

But nobody downstairs wanted to help me out. Seems I made <u>a big mistake</u> asking! Visiting Ladies Maids must do their own ironing—or the Midwinter staff are far too busy—or maybe they've just taken against me. After some very black looks & muttered words (muttered too low for me to hear thank goodness) I got passed along to a kitchen maid who said 'Best come with me.' She had a face like she'd sucked a lemon. I ran to keep up with her while she led the way thru a whole warren of rooms behind the Servants Hall.

I am getting the measure of the house now. Must be something like this:-

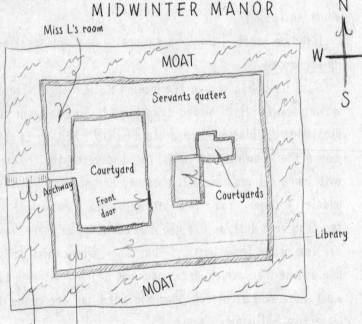

MIDWINTER MANOR

Miss L's room

MOAT

Servants quaters

Courtyard

Archway

Front door

Courtyards

N

W — E

S

Library

MOAT

Bridge   Lady S's room

At last she threw open a door & said 'The Ironing Room.' There was a long table padded with old sheets. Rows of irons ranging from toy-sized to huge & a fire to heat them on. The maid stuck a poker into the dying coals to get them aflame again—then she left me to it.

I must confess I have not had much practiss pressing fiddly cuffs & collars. Or indeed any practiss at all! What if I ruined Miss Lamb's good blouse? She hasn't got that many. Fashun Houses don't hand out free clothes to schoolteachers—only to big stars like Lily Lopez. I said to myself: just give it a go. Ironing can't be that hard. So I stuck the smallest iron on the fire & waited for it to warm up. Warmed myself at the same time. Thru the window I could see a small yard almost buried in snow. Snow clinging to the walls & all the overhangs & ledges. Never seen so much in my life!

While I was waiting someone muffled up in scarfs came out with a spade & began shovelling snow into a bucket. I made myself busy in case he could see me thru the glass. I spat on the iron to see how hot it was & spread out the blouse on the table. While my back was turned the scraping paused & I heard voices. They weren't very loud but I made out:-

'body'

& 'safe in there'

& 'cript'

& 'cold'.

Then someone sneezed & the voices stopped. Must confess I nearly burnt a hole in Miss Lamb's blouse while I was earwigging! Managed to take the iron off just in time.

My mind's been at work turning over those words:-
* A <u>body</u>—that means the poor gent I stumbled over.
* A <u>cript</u> is the cellar of a Church.
* A cript is always cold.
* So he's safe in there—it's a good place to store a body
  til the doctor or the funeral people arrive.
* Or <u>hide</u> a body!
* Sometimes bodies are buried in the cript (you see
  grave marker stones there).
* Does that mean they have <u>secretly buried</u> him already?

If they've buried him we will never discover the truth of
how the poor gent died!

I do wish Miss Lamb's Doctor James had got thru the
snowdrifts. He could look at the body & tell us what it was
that killed him. I keep thinking about it—but I still haven't
got a clue. Miss Kettle rushed me away so quick.

His face looked awfully DARK. That could be something
to do with what killed him. Or it may be his natural colour.
Or he may have lived abroad in a hot country til now. Or
was it the drink? But he didn't smell of drink—only of a
cold remedy like the one Gran uses.

There was NO BLOOD (not that I saw).

There was NO WEAPON (not that I saw) lying nearby.

But it was dim in the Libary & then it was crowded so any of them could have trampled over THE MURDER WEAPON without knowing.

Or trampled over it ON PURPOSE!! Kicked it out the way of prying eyes!?

Somebody must know something. But who?

LATER

Got lost trying to find my way back from the Ironing Room & had to beg help from a passing housemaid—the one that showed me to my room when I first got here. She's a bit younger & frendlier than the others. Said not to worry about them—everyone's in a bad mood cos there's too much to do & too few hands to do it. 'It's not even a big house-party. Not like the old days. We had lots more staff then. Now we get girls up from the village to help at busy times. But this snow has put a stop to that.'

She seemed glad to have a good old moan to me & I was glad to meet a kindly face. Her name is Edie Little. I shall remember that.

24 THE RED ROOM

Quentin expected his mother to be in shock, lying down with a cold compress over her eyes. Instead he found her seated at a dressing table, dabbing on face-powder. She looked remarkably composed. His father was nowhere to be seen.

'He's downstairs playing billiards,' Mrs Ives said. 'Or it may be upstairs. I simply cannot get the hang of this house. Well, he is *somewhere,* playing billiards with Marmaduke Roxburgh. There are no morning newspapers, you see.' She said that as if it was explanation enough.

Quentin took in the details of the Red Room. The bedcovers and curtains were of raspberry brocade and the walls papered in dark crimson. It was miles more luxurious than his own bedroom. He might as well have been put in the servants' quarters. The windows faced over the courtyard; they had a thick pile of snow against them but nothing like the icy coating upstairs. If this was the North Range, that explained it: his window must look northwards and the coldest winds always came from that direction.

His mother squinted at her reflection in the mirror. 'I had a dreadful night, and how it shows! Such a hard bed—still, it *is* a four-poster. I dare say dukes, and even queens, slept in it in days gone by. And those draughty old windowpanes. I awoke half-frozen.'

'Same here,' said Quentin. 'Then no one came to call me for breakfast, or light the fire. The house felt deserted. I thought I'd been abandoned.' He paused, gathering force. 'Mummy, we've got to go home!'

Their eyes met in the mirror. Mrs Ives' gaze was rather too glittery for Quentin's comfort.

'Don't be silly, darling. We can't go home. We were lucky to get here in all that snow, and we won't be able to leave in a hurry. Daddy simply will not want to chance his beloved motor car yet.'

'But, Mummy . . .'

His mother seemed not to have heard him. 'Besides, Daddy is just getting to know everyone, and Marmaduke Roxburgh is enormously well-connected. Anything might come of a chance like this!'

Quentin stared out at the courtyard. A manservant was chopping at the snow with an enormous shovel, trying to cut a pathway. If this was what it was like within the shelter of Midwinter Manor's high walls, what was it like outside?

'But Mummy,' he tried again, 'aren't you the least bit worried about—um—*events?*'

His mother stiffened. Her face became wary. 'Events, Quentin? What *can* you mean?'

'I mean a dead body in the library! Surely that doesn't happen at every house-party you go to?'

Mrs Ives laughed, not very convincingly.

'And unless he died of natural causes, someone must

be responsible for that death . . .'

'Quentin!'

'And if someone *is* responsible, where are they now?'

'Really, darling, I didn't think you'd have heard about it. I'd much rather you children knew nothing.'

'*Mother*. I'm not stupid.'

Mrs Ives turned round on her brocade-covered stool and faced Quentin. 'You really mustn't fret. It is a little unusual, I'll grant you. But rest assured, Lady Sleete has everything in hand.'

'A *little unusual*?' Quentin's tone was scathing. His mother saw nothing except what she wanted to see. She accepted what she was told and didn't delve below the surface. She was thrilled at the invitation to Midwinter Manor and nothing was going to stop her enjoying her visit. He tried another argument.

'Not only that, but some papers have been stolen from Cosway Otter's room. His top-secret plans! And now they think that *I*—'

Mrs Ives sighed dramatically. 'What nonsense, darling! Mr Otter said nothing about it at breakfast.'

Too busy scoffing all the sausages, thought Quentin. Honestly, parents—you couldn't rely on them for help! But then he knew that already.

He began to pace again, one hand in his dressing gown pocket, the other grasping its lapel, feeling more like Sherlock Holmes by the second. At least Mr Otter hadn't told the entire breakfast table about the theft. Quentin hadn't taken any papers, but they *were* missing; so unless it was a maid who'd moved them (he didn't even believe that theory himself) someone else had.

Nancy seemed to think the theft might be connected to the murder. If he couldn't go home yet, then at least he could do some detecting. And he couldn't do it alone.

Mrs Ives yawned delicately. 'I really think it's time I had a little snooze, darling. After the night I've had.'

Quentin took the hint and left.

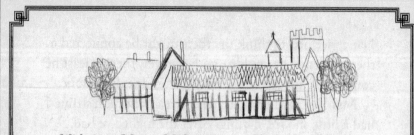

Midwinter Manor, Midwinter, near Tunbridge Wells, Kent

Dear N.

Not leaving after all. No one seems to be taking "the matter" seriously! Why ever not?

Need yr help. Broom cupboard. 12 sharp.

Yours, S. Holmes (!)

P.S. Destroy this note when you have read it.

25 THE ITEM IN QUESTION

NANCY'S JOURNAL

Just before servants' dinner was served—sharp at midday—
the Butler rapped on the table & announced he would 'say
a few words.' Grave faces all round. Even Sophie Leblonk
managed a serious expression—tho the dimple in her chin
always makes her look as if she is trying not to smile.

The Butler called it The Unfortunate Event That Has
Ockurred. He never said BODY or DEAD at all!

He told us that the Police & Medical Persons could not
as yet be reached. They were still waiting for the telephone
lines to be restored. Betts—that's Lady Sleete's driver—
had tried to get up the lane on foot without sucksess. The
snow was too deep. (Outside I could see snowflakes falling
thick & fast again.)

'So'—the Butler went on—'The Unfortunate Event is
being dealt with as well as can be. The <u>item-in-question</u>
has been taken care of. In all due course the Orthorities
will see to it. Your duty is not to worry about matters that
don't concern you but to go about your tasks as usual at
this busy time.'

What a way to talk!! The body of Mr Osmond Phipps—
or whoever it was—called an <u>item</u>. Made me think of Aunty
Bee's Lost Property Office & all those items that get
left behind. I was even more sorry for the poor man then.

Seemed like no one cared who the dead chap was or how he got that way <u>except me</u>. We were all being patted on the head & told to put it out of our minds. Just get on with our job of making the posh folks feel as comfortable as possible so it doesn't spoil Lady Sleete's plans. While the item-in-question is hidden in the cript (wherever that is) until the Orthorities get here.

Then supprise supprise! A voice beside me spoke up. Sophie Leblonk.

'Do you know oo the poor fellow is, Moos-ewer?' she said. 'Ow ee came to be in such a state? Can we rest in our beds safe & sound?'

A murmur went round the room. I could have hugged & kissed Sophie at that second.

The Butler wriggled a bit & said in a pompous voice 'The gentleman-in-question arrived to see Her Ladyship without an appointment.' As if that alone was enough to deserve ending up <u>lifeless on the floor</u>! 'On a private matter of bizness. He may have been ill. Or was affected by the extreme cold. A medical person could tell us more. But—alas—the snow.'

And that was all he would say.

Fortnum the Butler

26 SCARED

NANCY'S JOURNAL

Quentin can be so dim! I never got his note in time.
Servants aren't free to come & go like he is. Lucky I
tracked him down eating lunch in the dreary day nursery
on the top floor. I feel sorry for any Sleete children that
grew up there—& for their Nannies!

Quentin was bundled up like a sack of potatoes in a
long dressing gown. (He says he was cold.) But also seems
to think that's how Sherlock Homes looked.

Q.   How Q. sees himself

I was hoping to catch a glimpse of the Otter boy & girl too. But they'd eaten their lunch & gone outside. In this weather! Quentin pointed at a window 1/2 blocked by snow. Far below 2 shapes in woolly hats & scarves were trudging along the far side of the moat & every so often looking up at the house. According to Q. they are Utterly Cracked & not worth wasting time on.

Quentin says he's not leaving Midwinter Manor cos he can't perswade his mum & dad to go. Mrs Ives—usually quite a fussy lady—is not the least bothered that someone died here last night. Seems she is more concerned that Mr Ives can go on playing billiards & smoking cigars with all the BIGWIGS than running round shouting:-

'HELP!
We are stuck in a snowbound house
& someone here may have committed murder!
But who knows WHICH ONE?'

I told him the Butler had said much the same just now. That everything is in hand & not to worry our silly little heads about it! We agreed they are trying to sweep it under the carpet.

'They' means:-

Lady Sleete herself—it is her house & whoever came last night came to see her.

Mr Hawk the Lawyer.

The Butler—I bet he has been with Lady Sleete for years & years & prides himself on being UTTERLY LOYAL. He may even go as far as to break the law for her.

As for the rest of the servants—from what I've seen they do as they are told & beleeve whatever he tells them.

I said I had A Clue about the identity of Lady Sleete's visitor & whispered it into Quentin's ear. He was v. excited to hear that. 'Then who is he investigating?'

Was I said. Was. If I am right poor Osmond Phipps will do no more investigating in this life. His LIFELESS BODY is at this very moment lying in a Cript. Maybe he came with something Lady Sleete didn't like—or maybe he never got to tell her! Someone else did away with him just in time!!

We both went quiet then. It was cold & the house creaked & groaned in the wind. Not the best sir-cum-stances for making you feel brave. Quentin asked me if I was scared. I straitened my shoulders & said No! (For my own sake just as much as his.)

Cos I'm a very un-important young maidservant & he's just boy in a dressing gown. How could we possibly be the ones investigating a crime??!!

27 SOMETHING FISHY

NANCY'S JOURNAL

On my way back from meeting Quentin that slimy valet Nash stepped out from a dark corner & barred my way. Nearly jumped out of my skin! (So much for not being scared.)

He told me I had to follow him.

Now I knew that a proper Lady's Maid would be FURIOUS at someone else's valet trying to order her about. So I stuck out my chin & put on my best hoity-toity manner.

'I most certainly shall not,' I declared. 'You better explain yourself.'

'Sir Marmaduke Roxber would like a word with you. If you please,' he added all sarcastick.

'Oh would he indeed?' I went on. I was quite enjoying myself by then. Until he replied that it was about last night's discovery. I said I'd already spoken to Lady Sleete & prepared to walk away.

'Sir Marmaduke likes to keep himself informed.'

'Then Sir Marmaduke can ask Her Ladyship,' I said. I nearly added 'If they are such great chums'—but that might have been a bit too hoity-toity.

Then Nash said 'He would rather ask you' which made me stop. There was something FISHY about this. But I couldn't put my finger on it yet. So I told him—all very grashus—I dare say I could spare him 5 minutes.

Nash led me to a very out-of-the-way sitting room. Sir Marmaduke stood in front of the blazing fire looking stern. No shiny lapels & dimond pins today. He wore a country-fied tweed suit & I can only say the colour of it was <u>horse manure</u>. Like someone had pushed him over in the Dung Heap! (Look forward to telling them at home about that.) It was not much use me being hoity-toity with a Sir so I kept my eyes down, all very polite. When he glared at me I just kept telling myself about that dung heap.

Sir M. asked a lot of the same questions Mr Hawk did. Lady Sleete can't have told him a thing. Maybe they are <u>not close chums</u>.

Then he said I was un-natural calm last night—no hisstericks at all. Why was that? As if my lack of screaming & crying likely made me a Murderer. He is the sort who <u>thinks maids scream</u> if they drop a plate. He certainly expected Lady Sleete to have A FIT OF THE VAPOURS. (I can just hear Aunty Bee saying 'Men call women The Weaker Sex. Fat lot they know about it!')

So I told him I did shreek at first—to summon aid— but afterwards knew that more screeching would not help matters. Put that in your pipe & smoke it Sir Marmaduke!

Next he remarked in a nasty way that I was very young to be a personal maid. So I told him Miss Lamb was training me up. That she knew me from my schooldays & wanted to give me a start in life! (Thoght this was a good story. It helps if you stick close to the truth even when you are TELLING A LIE.) Sir M. muttered something about dragging me up from the London gutters!! If I could have clocked him one then I would—he deserved it. Making out that just cos I come from Bread Street behind the biscuit factory I must be raised in a Den of Theeves. The only reason I didn't smack him in the gob was I didn't want it to look bad for Miss Lamb.

He didn't even seem to notice.

Cos he went straight on to asking about PAPERS. Did I notice any papers? On the person of the deceased—or scattered nearby? I pretended to be as dim as he thoght I was & said there might have been a copy of The Times on the libary table.

He went on—'An envelope perhaps? Inside his coat?'

So did he mean the secret papers that Quentin was on about? (Except I think they were stolen during the night.) Or notes a Private Investigator would keep on the person they were investigating!? And had with them to show to Lady Sleete? (In that case was it Sir M. that he was looking into?)

I shook my head & looked stupid & scared & the questions came to an end. I'm sure he concluded I was just a silly girl. Being seen as a silly girl can be quite useful—no one ever suspects you have a sharp BRAIN in your head & that brain is working v. hard.

Funniest thing: as I was going out I saw in the corner an old-fashunned armchair—with a sort of carved hood for keeping out drafts—& full of blankets. I swear there was someone tucked deep inside. Cos I spied a wrinkled face & a pair of eyes twinkling away!! <u>Most peculiar.</u> Did Sir Marmaduke even know they were there? Listening to every word we said?

28 THE CASE OF
THE STOLEN PAPERS

The noblest path, Quentin decided, was to tackle the lion in his den. He worked out a speech and went over and over it in his head. Now he took a deep breath and knocked on Mr Otter's bedroom door. No answer. Quentin hesitated, knocked again, and was about to slide away when a voice inside said, 'Come in.'

Cosway Otter glanced up from his desk and smiled, which was odd. Mr Otter smiling in welcome at the main suspect in the Case of the Stolen Papers?

'You must be Quentin,' he said. 'If you're looking for Prescott and Berenice, you're out of luck.'

Really? Prescott Otter? Beans was short for Berenice? Quentin's mouth twitched. He hated his own name, sure enough, but *Prescott* and *Berenice*!

'I'm glad you're here, though…' Mr Otter continued, and Quentin felt a dizzy descent from the edge of laughter to the chill depths of fear.

'It wasn't me! I didn't even *know* about them!' Oh no, he really hadn't meant it to come out like that.

Mr Otter frowned. 'I was going to say I'm glad you're

here, as we haven't met many other children on our travels. Or not many that speak the same language. It's good for my two to have some company again.'

'Oh…'

'They told me all about your adventures last night. Cramming yourselves into—what is it, the priest's hole?—behind a moving panel.'

It didn't sound as if he knew *all* about their adventures. It wasn't just harmless fun, a silly game of Sardines.

'Um, no, Mr Otter, I'm not looking for Beans—Berenice, I mean—and, er, Prescott. It's *you* I came to see.' Quentin's heart was pounding so hard he felt it must show right through all his layers of clothes. Right, here goes. 'They told me this morning that something was stolen from your desk. I just wanted you to know, honestly, sir, it wasn't me.'

'You, Quentin?'

Mr Otter's face was a picture. He clearly thought that the idea of Quentin as a successful raider of secret documents was utterly ridiculous.

'Well, I . . . it's just that I . . . I might have had the opportunity. Last night. Of taking them. But I didn't. So now you know. Whatever anyone says.'

'I think you are safe from suspicion, Quentin. You certainly don't resemble my idea of an industrial spy.'

Mr Otter bent his head low over the paperwork on his desk and scribbled busily. It looked suspiciously as if he was trying to hide another smile.

Quentin felt hurt. Why *couldn't* he be an industrial spy? No one would suspect an ordinary schoolboy; it was the perfect cover. He might be working for someone else—Sir Marmaduke Roxburgh, for example, or his own father. Mr Otter hadn't thought of that, had he!?

Then Quentin remembered that he was supposed to be explaining his innocence. 'I would never stoop to such a thing. I'm a gentleman, and—and—an old friend of your niece Ella Otter, if you want proof. In fact, Ella and I did some investigating together, with some success. So I'm here to offer my services—'

Suddenly the door burst open and Beans and Scottie tore into the room, bringing the raw smell of outside with them. Their cheeks and noses were rosy-red. They shouted, 'We're frozen!'

'We got all round the house in the end!'

'We left our coats and boots to thaw downstairs!'

Beans was still wearing a snow-caked woolly hat. She plucked it off her head and hung it by the fire. Scottie sat down and tugged at his thick socks. 'No tracks that we could see, but then it's snowed a lot since.' He didn't seem to have noticed Quentin.

Quentin cleared his throat. 'Just been straightening out the little matter of the papers,' he said.

'You did?' asked Beans, her voice unsure.

Mr Otter looked pained. 'I was about to explain to Quentin that I've informed Lady Sleete, and she and I are looking into it. So there is an end to it, thank you, children.'

But there isn't an end! Quentin wanted to shout. Not yet. Not until the papers are found and the real thief unmasked.

'Who else knew about the papers, sir?' he asked.

Scottie butted in. 'Nobody. They were *secret* papers.'

'Ye-es, in that I've not shown them to anyone yet,' began Mr Otter. 'Of course, I've talked to people here about my work in general. In fact, I had a long discussion with Lady Sleete and Miss Lopez at our first lunch together. They were very interested.'

Aha! thought Quentin.

'But I think the ladies were just being kind. Rather than having any true understanding.'

Beans exploded. 'Dad! How can you say that? When you've *always* expected me to be just as capable and clever as my brother! I'm sure Lady Sleete has the brains to grasp it. And Miss Lopez, even if she's a musical comedy actress—'

'An actress,' Quentin suggested, 'can quite easily *act* at being a scatterbrain, when really she's very clever.'

Mr Otter held up the palms of his hands. 'Enough, enough. Please, leave this matter to the grown-ups.'

29 JIGSAW PUZZLE

NANCY'S JOURNAL

Next thing was to find Miss Lamb. I didn't have to look far. There's a parlour at the end of the West Range along from the Rose Room & that's where I heard voices. The door was open a touch so I peered in.

Miss Lamb, Mr Grant & someone who <u>had</u> to be Lily Lopez were round the fire doing a big jigsaw puzzle. Chatting like old friends. I tapped on the door—v. softly—& stepped just inside. Nobody noticed.

Lily Lopez is indeed STAR QUALITY. That lovely face & sleek blonde hair just makes you stop & stare. Then—her frock! Her shoes! Her sparkling rings! She's got a <u>carrying</u> sort of voice. (I'm sure that helps in the theatre—something else I must practiss.) I heard her say something about Lady Sleete.

'She wasn't going to let me wriggle out of coming here. Oh no! Sent her driver over specially to fetch me from Eden Castle.'

'Eden Castle!' Miss Lamb gasped as if v. impressed. Never heard of it myself.

Miss Lopez went on. 'Yesterday—before the snow began & everyone else arrived. We had a cozy lunch. Just Lady Sleete & Cosway Otter & me.' She waved at the window. 'But look at it now. We shall <u>never escape</u>!' (I must say she is very DRAMATIC.)

Mr Grant put in 'You scarcely thoght something nasty would happen next' & Lily said 'No! It's the kind of thing you only find in a book. You must put it in your next one Jasper.'

Miss Lamb added 'Or a play. Then Lily can star in it.'

I was dying to ask 'And if there could be a part in it for a Maid? Just a few words—opening a door—or holding a teatray?' The next step of my Acting Career! (Forgetting all about my Detective career!!)

I was GLUED TO THE SPOT at being so close to Famous People (not just talking about books & plays—but books & plays they wrote & starred in!) when someone came in at the far end of the room. I slid back into the shadows cos I knew that voice: Lady Sleete. She asked—but really ordered—'dear Jasper' to come & play the piano & 'dear Lily' to sing for the guests. Jasper said he was rather rusty while Lily made a sulky face only Miss Lamb (& me) could see. But they got up & went all the same. Leaving Miss L. all alone with the jigsaw puzzle. Lady Sleete did not ask her.

I stepped forward & Miss L. jumped. Put her hands to her heart. Said how she had been dreading this visit to James's grandmother but nothing could have prepared her for how grim it was turning out. Everyone goes about acting so calm & sofisticated—but underneath they are really RATTLED.

She wanted to know how I got on this morning so I told her about Lady Sleete's lawyer & the grilling he gave me. (Didn't go into my run-in with Sir Marmaduke just now—still chewing that over.) She said 'Henry Hawk?? He's a strange old bird—I met him at dinner last night. He was late arriving. We'd sat down at table before he came in.'

Late! Was he now!? Cos Quentin heard 2 men talking in the libary when dinner <u>was underway</u> & I am trying to work out who those men were.

Miss Lamb remarked that he was probbly held up by the snow. But when I spelled it out she was Horrorfied all over again. She said 'If there was any Foul Play then it is A MATTER FOR THE POLICE. Until they get here you <u>must not</u> do anything to put yourself in danger. I simply cannot let you! What would your family say?'

(Well—Gran would declare she never wanted me to take this job in the 1st place & Aunty Bee would say 'Nancy is <u>always</u> drawn to danger—there's no stopping her!' Dad is a man of few words. Heaven knows what he'd think.)

I explained I was merely <u>Compiling a list of Suspeckts</u> & pointed to the jigsaw puzzle. Told her that you've got to get all the bits in the right place & sometimes a bit of green grass looks the same as a bit of green tree. Until you try it & find it doesn't fit!

Rather a clever way of putting things. If I say so myself.

And that's where Miss Lamb comes in. I wasn't round that dinner table last night—& nor was that stuck-up Quentin Ives. I didn't see who came & went. Or hear what they said. But Miss Lamb did. So very politely I asked her to write down exactly what she witnessed & anything else about Lady Sleete's guests that comes to mind.

30 BEING METHODICAL

NANCY'S JOURNAL

Since Lady Sleete had got her visitors (except Miss L.) busy singing round the Piano I <u>took my chance</u> & went back for another look at the Libary. The room was bitter-cold & deadly silent. Dusk was coming on & the snow outside threw an un-earthly light into the place. Very spooky! Specially when you remember that last night a Body was lying right here.

I worked from one end to the other. It is called being METHODICAL. That way you don't miss anything. Not that there was anything to miss. No bloodstains on the rugs or the floorboards. No hidden weapons—or not that I could find. Apart from book-shelves & tables & chairs there is little in the way of fuss & fol-der-olls like some folk choose to have about their houses. The only hiding places were in among the books. I didn't have time to take down each & every book in the room to check. There must be hundreds! I had to look for something more obvius.

Besides—sometimes in a Detective Story <u>the clue everyone is looking for</u> turns out to be the thing that was STARING THEM IN THE FACE all along!

On the first mantelshelf there were two silver candlesticks (with fresh candles in) & a brass statue of a horse. You could hit someone over the head with <u>any of them</u>! I had a quick look but there weren't any dents or marks on them. The horse was v. heavy but also small & hard to get a good grip on. (I am thinking like a MURDERER now!!) I took one of the candlesticks & waved it about a bit. Tried to work out just how an attacker would hit with it.

sharp downward blow

deadly weapon

come up
behind
victim

silent feet

Thank Heavens it was really dark by then so nobody was able to see me from outside. Sir Marmaduke & Mr Hawk would certainly have a few more questions to ask me if they knew! But:-

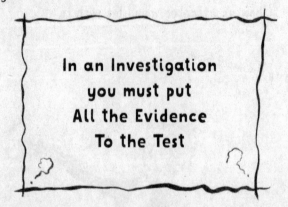

**In an Investigation
you must put
All the Evidence
To the Test**

I set that candlestick back as careful as I could & wiped it with my hankerchief first so there are no black marks on the silver for any housemaid to find later.

On the mantelshelf at the far end of the libary there was just 1 candlestick. Which got me thinking. Had there been <u>a pair</u> there yesterday? Had someone taken the 2nd one away? Hidden it? Or thrown it in the Moat? Which got me thinking even harder. The Moat is the <u>perfect place</u> for chucking stuff in. It is right below the windows & no one would ever look in it. Except then I remembered that the Moat was FROZEN OVER & probbly had been last night too. Anything lobbed out a window would still be lying there on top of the ice—tho today's snow would have covered it up by now.

Besides that 1 single candlestick there were 2 china dogs sitting facing each other —spaniels by the look of it—+ a fancy tin. The tin only had cough drops inside. Someone had left it there on the end of the mantleshelf. (Didn't Quentin say one of the men he heard had a cough!?) You couldn't hit someone over the head with a cough drop tin. Or with a China Spaniel—not without breaking it.

Time was getting on & I was scared someone would come in. But I could not resist having a go at finding the end of that Secret Passage. As a housemaid I was much ackwainted with plaster & panels & walls & wainscots since it was my job to keep the blasted stuff clean. I know what they sound like as you knock against them with a broom & dust them with a cloth. I know when they sound SOLID & when they sound HOLLOW. I had a quick trip round the wooden panels tapping with the back of my nuckles as I went. And so I found—to the right of the far fireplace—a hollow sound! Easy when you know how. (Can't wait to report that back to Quentin Ives.)

Following my search of the Library this is my <u>Theory</u>:-
* Method of Murder—??? hit with heavy object
* Murder Weapon—??? missing candlestick
* Evidence of Blood from head wound—none.

    Of course it is just a Theory at the moment. If only I
could get into the Cript (wherever that is) & see the Corpse.

News about the S****t P****ge!

+ <u>more</u>!!

Meet usual place. Will try to get away for 8 p.m.
If not poss leave another note here.

N.P.

31 A STUDENT OF HUMAN NATURE

Dashing through the West Range after visiting Mr Otter, Quentin crossed an empty sitting room and found it wasn't empty, after all. Lamb-and-Mint-Sauce was tucked away in a wing chair, writing.

'Quentin!' she called out. 'Not attending this afternoon's entertainment?'

He had to stop. 'The—?'

'Miss Lopez is singing, with Mr Grant accompanying her on the piano. In the big drawing room, if you want to find them.'

'I'm not really a singing sort of chap.'

Lamb-and-Mint-Sauce gave him a sympathetic smile. 'What sort of a chap are you, then? Do you like puzzles?'

There was an unfinished jigsaw puzzle on the table in front of her. Grudgingly, Quentin glanced down at it. Half a unicorn, the head of a lion, a mass of flowery grass, and lots of gaps. He slid one glaringly-obvious piece into place, and then another. 'Prefer reading, actually,' he murmured.

'Wonderful!' Miss Lamb smiled even more broadly.

She nudged a few more puzzle pieces his way, so that he could complete the corner. While he was occupied she put the cap on her pen and folded her writing paper carefully, making it into a long narrow slip which she tucked inside her sleeve. 'I'm a great reader myself and it's always good to find like-minded people. What kind of books do you like best?'

'Adventures. Spies. Sherlock Holmes.'

'Sherlock Holmes? I've read a great many of those stories myself.'

Quentin coughed modestly and said, 'I myself am what you might call a student of human nature. Like Mr Holmes, I observe, and analyse what I see.'

Lamb-and-Mint-Sauce nodded. 'Let's see. What have you observed about me?'

This was rather a good test. He'd show her.

'You like the colour green.'

'Do I?'

'Yes. You're wearing green now, and also at breakfast, though not the same dress—blouse—thing.'

'That's true.'

'You have a spot of ink on your right forefinger. You have recently been writing and secreted a paper in your sleeve.'

Her eyes sparkled. 'That's cheating! You saw me do it.'

'Yes,' Quentin agreed. He stuck his hands in his pockets and strolled about; it made thinking much easier. 'But even if I hadn't, there's the ink, and half an inch of folded paper showing at your cuff. Why would someone fold a letter into a strip, instead of in half crossways, unless they wanted to keep it hidden? You only thought of hiding it, and hiding it in your sleeve, *after* you had written it—so you didn't want *me* to see it.'

'You have well and truly found me out!' Miss Lamb declared. Oddly, she looked pleased. 'Now, tell me what you've observed about the others. Starting with Lady Sleete…'

Quentin had to admit he had barely laid eyes on her. She was there to greet his parents, but he was taken up to the children's quarters right away.

'Sir Marmaduke Roxburgh, then?'

He had nothing nice to say about Sir Marmaduke, but did Miss Lamb want to hear that? Was she a friend of his? Would he get himself into trouble with his opinions? He studied her face, and began, 'He's the sort of man who steals a marble from a child…'

'And how precisely do you work that out?'

'I saw him do it.'

'Really? When?'

'Yesterday. He took Beans Otter's best marble from her—just snatched it—and would not give it back. He pretended it was a joke, but it wasn't. I would say that makes him a bully.'

'How strange. Marmaduke Roxburgh is terribly rich, and has the ear of all sorts of powerful people. He can do whatever he wants. Why ever would he need to steal a child's marble?'

Quentin remembered something else then. That Sir Marmaduke took Beans's marble from her in *the library*, and after that he hurried them out, saying that he was due to meet with Lady Sleete there. He said they did not wish to be disturbed, by anyone! Supposing he was due to meet with *the dead man* as well?

Miss Lamb interrupted these thoughts. 'I see I can trust your instincts, Quentin. Would you like to help me? I know you're not a singing sort of chap, but would you go along to the big drawing room now and observe Lady Sleete for me? I'd very much like to hear what you have to say about our hostess. I feel she's been rather unkind to me, but of course I may be misjudging her.'

Unkind to good old Lamb-and-Mint-Sauce, who seemed the soul of kindness herself? Quentin tightened his dressing gown cord and smoothed his lapels. With a determined, wordless nod, he set off.

32 MISS LAMB'S ACCOUNT

NANCY'S JOURNAL

Miss Lamb did what I asked! Came back before dinner with it all written out & keen to hear anything new I'd picked up. I shall put it in here.

Midwinter Manor, Midwinter, near Tunbridge Wells, Kent

Nancy, it seems very strange writing all this down on Lady Sleete's own notepaper, although it's the only thing that came to hand. Do keep it safe from prying eyes.

A.L.

Lady Sleete (head of the table)

Sir Marmaduke Roxburgh

Cosway Otter

Lily Lopez

Mrs Ives

Mr Ives

Jasper Grant

Miss Kettle

Princess Canova

myself

Henry Hawk

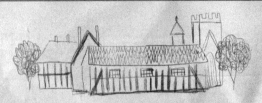

Midwinter Manor, Midwinter, near Tunbridge Wells, Kent

I wonder where James would have sat, had he been here? I felt that all the 'interesting' people were placed together near Lady Sleete, and I was seated at the 'dull' end of the table.

Towards the end of the meal the butler had a word with Lady Sleete about the snowstorm, after which Miss Kettle went off to make arrangements for Mr Hawk to stay the night. He lives a mile or two away in Lower Winter.

Thus it was Lady Sleete, Princess Canova, Mrs Ives, Lily, and I who went to the Drawing Room to take our coffee. As far as I know, Sir Marmaduke, Mr Otter, Mr Grant, Mr Ives, and Mr Hawk remained in the Dining Room.

The rest you know, as I described it to you that night when I came up.

Now for my observations of my fellow-guests . . .

I have really warmed to Lily Lopez. She is wonderfully down-to-earth for someone so famous, not to mention beautiful. In addition she likes to gossip, which is fun, since she knows everyone there is to know; and her gossip is amusing rather than malicious. I hope I have not been utterly taken in by her charm!

Midwinter Manor, Midwinter, near Tunbridge Wells, Kent

From Lily I learned that Princess Canova is a distant cousin of the Sleetes. The name and title are from her husband. Princes & Dukes are two-a-penny where he came from, according to Lily. But the Prince is long dead and the land and castles gone. The Princess returned to England at the start of the War, penniless. She takes turns living with different relatives. She is tiny and wizened like a marmoset monkey, and terribly deaf, which makes it difficult to converse with her.

Jasper Grant is well-known for his books and plays. He seems to be one of those people who gets on easily with everyone, and it helps that he makes rather a joke of his literary success. I'm sure Lady Sleete invites him here often because he is such good company.

Sir Marmaduke Roxburgh, on the other hand, strikes me as one of those overbearing, puffed-up men. He may well be important but he needs everyone to know it. He likes to attach his name to things: apparently there's a Roxburgh cup for horse racing, sailing, and so on. Insufferable!

In contrast I found Mr Cosway Otter thoughtful and soft-spoken, not at all what I expected from an American. I

Midwinter Manor, Midwinter, near Tunbridge Wells, Kent

suspect he is much, much cleverer than he lets on.

I know nothing about <u>Mr & Mrs Ives</u>. He's a 'business' type and she is a little starry-eyed about the other guests.

<u>Miss Kettle</u>, Lady Sleete's companion, seems pleasant and well-meaning though kept very busy by all her duties. I imagine that Lady Sleete must drive her mad at times.

<u>Henry Hawk</u> is very old-fashioned and formal. He appeared distant and distracted at dinner. I feel that our small-talk annoyed him, for he barely chatted with the ladies at his end of the table. He tried some serious business with Mr Ives about land and property, but Mr Ives only wanted to talk about golf.

My goodness, Nancy, I have rather enjoyed penning these character studies for you. Perhaps I shall 'make a detective' after all!

♥

33 A LIST

NANCY'S JOURNAL

(Based on Miss Lamb's account & my own evidence)

PEOPLE WHO COULD NOT POSSIBLY HAVE COMMITTED MURDER LAST NIGHT:

Princess Canova—is too old & too tiny to murder a grown man.

Mr & Mrs Ives—I can't bileve Quentin's parents have come here to murder someone. Q. says his mum does charity work with Lady Sleete, & his dad wasn't keen on coming to Midwinter until he found the billiard room & Sir M. to chat to.

The indoor servants—busy in the Kitchen or Dining Room or both all night long with other people always around.

Miss Lamb (of course).

I want to add Miss Kettle (as she's been kind to me) but she left the Dining Room & who knows what she did after that? Supposed to be sorting out the Lawyer's room & would probbly take a housemaid with her for that. But when I ran out of the Library she was the 1st person I met—& she was ALONE.

PEOPLE WITH AN ALIBI
& LOTS OF WITNESSES TO SAY
WHERE THEY WERE:

Lady Sleete
Sir Marmaduke
L. Lopez
J. Grant
Cosway Otter

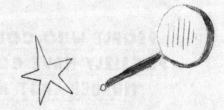

Which leaves:

PEOPLE WHO ACTUALLY COULD HAVE
COMMITTED MURDER AS NOBODY
KNOWS WHERE THEY WERE:-

Mr Hawk (he was late for dinner)

Miss Kettle (she left early)

Sophie Leblonk

Nash—Sir M.'s valet Betts—Lady S.'s driver.
  (Almost forgot about him!)

Which also leaves ME! I know where I was—but nobody
  else does for sure. (A bit tricky.)

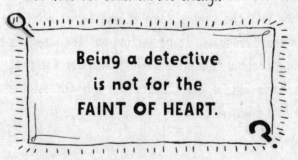

Being a detective
is not for the
FAINT OF HEART.

34 ALL UTTERLY CRACKED

Quentin was too late for the singing. He found a drawing room with a grand piano in it and a circle of empty seats. Except that one seat *wasn't* empty. The only person left was a wrinkled old creature, swathed in so many shawls she seemed buried by them. When she spied Quentin she beckoned him over and raised an ear trumpet. It looked like a cross between a musical instrument and a tobacco pipe. 'I'm a little hard of hearing,' she bellowed.

I'm not, thought Quentin.

'I must have dozed off for a moment or two. Where have they all gone?'

Quentin spoke carefully into the mouth of the ear trumpet. 'Wish I knew. I'm looking for Lady Sleete myself. Do you want me to find her for you?'

That would make a good excuse for tracking her down.

'Very kind, young man. But no, I see quite enough of Lady Sleete every day, thank you. Whereas the others—that enchanting singer, and amusing Mr Grant—ah well.'

The old lady rearranged her shawls and settled herself even more deeply into her nest. So he left her to it. The house rattled in the wind; beyond the windows snow fell unceasing. Everyone had disappeared again. They might have gone to their rooms to nap, or to change into yet another set of clothes . . . or something more sinister. Was one of them lurking suspiciously behind a closed door, waiting to strike? It wasn't just the cold that made the hairs rise on the back of his neck.

Courage! You can do it, he said to himself.

Poking his head into the billiard room, he found a lone man. He wasn't playing, just leaning against the billiard table, smoking a cigar. When he saw Quentin he seemed to jolt out of a daze. 'Anything I can do for you, old chap?'

'Have you seen Lady Sleete, please, sir?'

The man made a pantomime of peering round the room. 'Hmm…no…not in here. Awfully sorry.'

If that was meant to be funny, it was pretty lame. Then a thought occurred. 'Are you Jasper Grant, the author?'

The man nodded. He puffed on his cigar and blew out a perfect smoke ring. Quentin watched in awe as it floated away to the ceiling.

'And who might you be?'

'Quentin Ives.'

'Ah, son of Godfrey Ives, I presume?'

'Geoffrey,' Quentin mumbled.

Jasper Grant stuck his arms out and mimed an aeroplane careening through the sky, then brought his hands together as if on the steering wheel of a motor car. Quentin just stared at him. What on earth was he doing that for? Cracked. They were All. Utterly. Cracked.

But he had real live author in front of him, so he had to ask, 'What sort of thing do you write, Mr Grant?'

'Oh, tosh. Absolute tosh.'

Quentin knew he was meant to laugh at that, too.

'Do you ever write detective stories?'

'No. People are always telling me what I should put in my next book. Damn cheek. I take no notice.'

Quentin wasn't impressed. This fellow wouldn't be able to write anything half as good as a Sherlock Holmes story. He probably wrote slushy love stuff. *That's* why Mummy was so thrilled to meet him.

'Why are you after Lady Sleete, by the way?'

'Oh—um—.' Quentin knew that a good rule for spies was to hide in plain sight, so he gave the true explanation. 'I just wanted to see what she was like.'

Jasper Grant tapped the side his nose. 'Word of advice—keep your distance. Her Ladyship is not at all keen on kids. She's the old-fashioned type, thinks children should be seen and not heard. Ideally, not even seen.'

'Ah.'

'Now, cut along, there's good chap. It must be nearly time for your tea.'

35 THE ENGLISH SPIRIT

The last person Quentin came across was his mother, sitting at a writing table in a lamplit alcove. He tried to back away but too late—she had spotted him.

'I'm just dashing off one or two letters to friends. It's been a most marvellous afternoon. Imagine, Lily Lopez sang just for us! Though of course the poor dear Princess couldn't have heard a thing. She's deaf as a post, you know.'

'Who is?' asked Quentin.

'Princess Canova. The Canovas are old Italian nobility, I believe.'

'She didn't *sound* Italian.'

Mrs Ives was blotting a sheet of Midwinter Manor writing paper. Her head shot up. 'Have you met the Princess?'

Quentin nodded.

'When? Where?'

'In the drawing room just now. She said I was a very kind young man.'

'I should hope so. But *I* didn't see you at the musical recital, Quentin.'

'Wasn't there. It was after.'

'I'm pleased you made the right impression. It is so

important, when one is in good society— Quentin! What *on earth* are you wearing?'

Quentin smoothed down his dressing gown. 'Just—um—trying to keep warm, that's all. You said yourself this was an awful draughty old house.'

'Good Lord, I hope the Princess didn't see you in that? Where is your smart jacket?'

'In the bedroom cupboard.' Which wasn't an actual lie. It just wasn't in his bedroom cupboard *here*.

Fortunately his mother couldn't wait to share some more good news. 'Her Ladyship has wonderful plans for New Year's Eve. I understand that the children are allowed to join in, too.'

Quentin felt a cold horror in the pit of his stomach.

'Join in with what?'

'Playing Charades. It's a New Year's Eve tradition at Midwinter Manor.'

A dead body lay somewhere in the house and a thief had snatched vital papers from under their noses, yet all his mother *and* Lady Sleete could think about were party games! Quentin gritted his teeth and said through clenched jaws, 'Mummy. What if tomorrow, at long last, the police get through the snow? They arrive to investigate a mysterious death. And what do they find? Everyone playing charades! How will that look?'

'It will look as if we are all being brave in the face of adversity and trying to pass the time in the jolliest way we know. It is the English spirit. Besides, they haven't been summoned yet. No one can reach them by telephone and no one can get up or down that steep lane to the manor. And still it snows!'

Quentin wondered if his mother hadn't gone a bit nuts. She'd caught it from everyone else here.

'Doesn't that scare you the least little bit, Mummy?'

Mrs Ives shook her head. 'Not when Her Ladyship has assured us that matters are in hand.' Then she rolled her eyes and said in a half-whisper, 'But guess what I've heard? The man found in the library was a private detective!'

Which was what Nancy had said, too.

'Where did you get that from?'

'Princess Canova told me, in confidence.'

'But how would she know? You said she's as deaf as a post.'

'Just a manner of speaking, Quentin. I may have exaggerated a touch.' Mrs Ives hurried on. 'A private detective, though. That's a slippery sort of character. Hardly surprising if something dreadful befalls that type of man.'

'*What?* Sherlock Holmes is a private detective! Are you saying that he's a slippery character?'

Mrs Ives turned back to her letters, folding the sheets of paper and stuffing them into their envelopes. 'Really, Quentin. Now you're just being silly. Sherlock Holmes *is* a character—a made-up storybook character.' She stuck on a stamp and thumped it flat with the side of her fist. 'And didn't someone try to *do away* with Mr Holmes? Pushed him over a waterfall, wasn't it? So there you are.'

36 TRUCE

'Quentin? D'you mind if I come in?'

Before he could say yes or no, Beans was in his bedroom. She pressed the door shut and stood in front of it as if to stop him escaping.

Quentin didn't move. He was reading a comic and fixed on it as if it was the most riveting thing in the world. Without looking up he said, 'What d'you want?'

'I've come to apologize. I'm sorry that I ever thought you were the thief. Truce?'

Quentin just grunted.

Beans went on eagerly, as if he'd given his wholehearted consent. 'Listen, about earlier. My dad may have sounded as if he wasn't anxious about the stolen papers, that he and Lady Sleete have it all under control—well, that's not true. When he *doesn't* sound worried, that's when he really *is* worried. He just never likes to show it. He thinks it's better to present a calm face to the world.'

Quentin held his head. It ached from everything his mother had said, and Miss Lamb, and now this. 'So, let's see, your father's worried out of his mind about the missing papers even though he looks perfectly—'

Beans danced about impatiently. 'Yes, yes! So he

really does need our help, even if he denies it. That's why Scottie and I were outside earlier. We wanted to see if there were any other ways in and out of the manor, despite the moat, that a thief might take. If there were any tracks still visible despite the new snow.'

'Find anything?'

'Nothing useful. It was hard-going. Your English snow's so wet—you kind of sink down into it all the time.'

A picture came suddenly into Quentin's mind. A figure floundering through the snow: the one he'd seen below as he hung his head out of Mr Otter's bedroom window last night. The dark figure who seemed to be fleeing from the library! How could he have forgotten that? He ought to let Nancy know as soon as possible. He and Nancy were the professionals around here, not foolish amateurs like the Otter children. He swung himself off the bed.

'To be perfectly honest, Beans, I've other things on my plate just now.'

Beans sighed, then perked up. 'That reminds me! Miss Kettle asked me to fetch you for tea.'

'But there's something urgent I must—'

'Miss Kettle is nice enough, but she's really terribly strict underneath.'

And Quentin realized that he was really terribly hungry.

'What have you been up to this afternoon? Beans? Quentin?'

Quentin noticed that Miss Kettle didn't call Beans Berenice. That was one point in her favour.

Beans said nothing, so Quentin did the same. Scottie, on the other side of the table, was too busy eating to speak. Miss Kettle tried to tease some conversation out of them. 'This beastly weather. I expect you're all tired of being shut inside?'

'Oh, we went outside,' Beans said. 'The snow lasts for months where we live. You can't stay indoors all winter.'

Miss Kettle turned her sharp eyes on Quentin. 'Did you have fun?'

Quentin mumbled something about not having the right kind of boots with him.

'There may be some here that would fit,' Miss Kettle told him. 'I will look into it.'

Please don't, thought Quentin. He wasn't the outdoors type.

Miss Kettle began slicing a fruit cake. 'I wonder if any of you would care to help me with an errand tomorrow morning?'

'I shall be busy, I'm afraid,' Quentin said, thinking of the numerous strands of his investigation. But Miss Kettle went on as if he hadn't opened his mouth.

'Good. You will be required to walk some way, but you won't be needing boots.'

37 UNSUITABLE HABITS

NANCY'S JOURNAL

Just coming out of the Rose Room & ran into Sophie Leblonk. No time like the present to do little more Detecting—so I reminded her of her promise. She took me into Lily Lopez's bedroom where I pretended to admire the silk & velvet gowns with their matching bits & bobs. There were so many of them. Far too many for 3 days. Even with all the fussy changes of clothes they do here. Then I recalled that Lily had come straight here from Eden Castle. Must have stayed there for Christmas & it wouldn't do for a big star to turn up in the same outfit twice. (No idea how grand Eden Castle is. But it sounds even grander than Midwinter Manor!) I said as much to Sophie.

She looked blank for a moment then said 'Oh it is VAIRY grand' & quickly changed the subject by making me sniff at all Lily's bottles of scent on the dressing table. They were loveliest things I've ever smelled! I didn't dare dab any on in case somebody like Miss Kettle or the Butler got a wiff of me wearing scent. A most ~~UNSUT~~ UNSUITABLE HABIT for a maid. It isn't my place to go around smelling of Roses or Orange Blossom. Coal tar soap & cotton starch more like.

Then Sophie shocked me by picking up the bottle of perfume she said cost the most—pounds & pounds for a tiny drop—and dabbed it behind her ears. Grinning like mad as she did it. I said 'Good greef! You'll have to keep out of everyone's way all night' & she just laughed saying 'Cinderella is going to the ball!'

Knows her place

Unsuitable habits

Maybe it's cos she's French. Or cos working for a Famous Actress is <u>very different</u> from being maid to someone like Lady Sleete or any of the other ladies here.

Sad to say I couldn't get anything out of Sophie as to her whereabouts last night. She ignored me & went on & on about the new play Lily Lopez is to star in. Says it will be 'very modern' & would really be better for an actress with a stronger voice than Lily's got. (Sounding jellous again!) (Maybe—like me—she'd rather be an actress than a maidservant.) Said Lily is best at 'light fluff' & this part needs more <u>range</u>. I know from my <u>previous</u> Acting <u>experiense</u> (even if only in Sunday School plays) that means someone who can do lots of DIFFERENT MOODS.

Back in the Rose Room I practissed doing different moods in front of the big mirror. Before I knew it Miss Lamb was there to change for dinner. I should have been writing all this down instead!

157

38 MY LATEST THEORY

NANCY'S JOURNAL

Just had a mad meeting with Quentin. It's all so cumplicated my head is spinning. But that is <u>why a Good Detective makes notes</u>. There is so much to put down here I will need a new notebook soon!

1. Quentin said his Mum heard that the murder victim was a Private Investigator too! So I showed him the card I found—now it IS proof.

2. Cosway Otter has let him off over the stolen papers—tho Q. is still fuming that Mr Otter didn't think he'd be capable of taking them. (Typical Quentin.)

3. Q.'s theory is that Marmaduke Roxber is behind the theft—he's after Mr Otter's best ideas. Can't say I agree.

4. Miss Lamb (!) has asked Q. <u>to spy on Lady Sleete</u> for her. He says it's cos SHE DOES see him as a splendid undercover type & sharp-witted as Sherlock Holmes.

5. I don't know why Miss L. asked Quentin & NOT ME. He says he can go where I can't cos I'm just a maid.

6. But he didn't know I was <u>Miss Lamb's</u> lady's maid!! So much for him being sharp. He's clueless about servants altogether.

7. But—which makes up for that—he reckons he saw

someone running away from the Libary the night of the murder. He was looking out of Mr Otter's window just above.

I could hardly get a word in edgeways round all this. Told him about my trip to the libary tho & what I found there—& what he should look for if he dares go in. He seems to think someone went UP the secret passageway to steal the papers. Which is rubbish. This is why:-

- I was there when Marmaduke Roxber came into the Libary & he didn't know who the dead man was. (Didn't look like an act to me.)
- Did he only find out later who the Victim was? (Like Quentin's mum did.)
- Cos next day he wanted to know if I saw any papers when I found the body. According to Quentin Mr Otter's papers got stolen in the night. So Sir M. can't have been asking about the same ones.

Now we know the Dead Body really is Osmond Phipps—this brings me to My Latest Theory:-

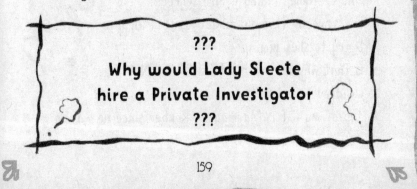

???
Why would Lady Sleete
hire a Private Investigator
???

To find out all about someone. That could be anyone in her life. I wouldn't know where to begin.

<u>But</u> (here it gets good) Phipps came to see her yesterday just as visitors were arriving for the New Year house-party. Makes sense that it was something to do with one of them. It was a horrible night. He wouldn't travel if he didn't have to. Lady Sleete needed to know urgently—or Phipps wanted to reach her urgently.

So it was about someone who is here now! Lady Sleete always invites <u>famous</u> and <u>important</u> people. She likes to be the one who puts them together & makes things happen—like putting A MATCH TO A FIREWORK.

So who could she be digging up the dirt on? What was she going to do with it??

Most likely it is one of those famous & important people. (Cos there would be nothing to find out about an ordinary soul like Miss Lamb.) My Grandma says we should always look up to our betters—but Aunty Bee says 'Codswallop! They're no better than us. Some are a lot worse!' So:-

- One of them's hiding <u>a dire secret!</u>
- Did someone find out about Osmond Phipps & try to shut him up?
- Is that why he met his TERRIBLE END (whatever it was)?
- Top of my list is <u>Marmaduke Roxber</u> since he was so

keen to grill me about what I'd seen—& whether there were papers on the body—& he didn't trust Lady Sleete to tell him!!

39 A NEW SIDE TO MISS LAMB

NANCY'S JOURNAL

I got no chance to ask Miss Lamb about why she asked
Quentin Ives—or anything else. For when she came to
bed she flung herself down crying 'Pansy Roxber! Pansy
Roxber! I am sick & tired of Pansy Roxber!!'

I am certainly seeing a new side to her—nothing like
the straight-laced straight-faced schoolteacher I used to
know. She must have had too much to drink at dinner. I
KNOW THE SIGNS. (In a maidservant's job you get to see
a lot!) First people grow very chatty—then all of a sudden
they get tired & cross. Miss Lamb was at the talking-too-
much stage. But I didn't know who she was talking about.
Pansy Roxber is not in any of my notes.

'Didn't know she was staying here,' I said.

To which Miss Lamb replied 'She isn't! But Lady Sleete
must have said her name 20 times tonight. 50 times! We
never heard the end of it. How much fun—how clever—how
original she is.'

Seems Pansy is Marmaduke Roxber's daughter. Lady
Sleete was itching to get her along to Midwinter too. But
Pansy turned the invite down.

Miss Lamb lay there—crushing her frock (Miss ~~Bown~~

Beaumont's best velvet)—& counting off on her fingers: 'Pansy is full of high spirits. Pansy can dance all night long. Pansy drives fast motor cars. Even races them! And that's not all—now she is learning to <u>fly a plane</u>!'

She let out the biggest sigh & clutched her head. 'And there was I—a dull little mouse in a borrowed dress stuck down at the wrong end of the table.'

I reminded her that at least she'd got a good friend in Lily Lopez. But she said Lily had a sore throat from singing & slipped away early.

I managed to get Miss Lamb off the bed & out of that dress so I could give it a good shake & hang it up. She paced up & down saying 'Of course what Lady Sleete really means is that she'd much rather James got engaged to Pansy Roxber than a trifling little Nobody like me. Pansy is brave & dashing—not to menshun VERY VERY RICH. The kind of girl the Heir to the Sleetes <u>should</u> marry. She's perfect.'

So that was it. Miss Lamb's mind was a-wirl with horrid thoghts—but by then so was <u>mine</u>.

I bet Lady Sleete invited Pansy so that Doctor James could see her side-by-side with Miss Lamb. So that Pansy could turn his head with her all-night dancing & tales of motor races & air-o-plane flying. Lady Sleete hoped to <u>throw a spanner in the works</u>. No wonder she never introduced Miss Lamb as her grandson's ~~feeons~~ fiancée. She's keeping that quiet & Miss Lamb dare not utter a word about it before Dr James gets here. Thank heavens Pansy Roxber had somewhere more fun to be than Midwinter Manor.

When Miss L. came out of the bathroom she seemed a bit calmer—but still full of the effects of wine—for throwing herself onto the bed she said 'I'm quite ex-orsted. D'you know—I went for a long long walk today? With a little dog!' It's hardly the weather for long walks so I thoght she was <u>talking nonsense</u>. But turns out it was with Miss Kettle in some Long Gallery along the top of the West Range. 'We kept going up & down. Just like ladies back in olden times—stretching their legs when they could not go outside in the muck and the wet. We had such an interesting chat.'

So <u>what</u> did they chat about? (Miss Kettle must be party to all sorts of secrets!) Miss L. just yawned & crawled under the covers. Mumbling about the Long Gallery—& all the Sleete portraits there—& something about rumours of a secret passage. I tried to ask. But her eyes were shut & her mouth fallen open.

40 ALL DRESSED UP

NANCY'S JOURNAL

Writing this sitting up in bed in my own room. I don't fancy another night on that couch & Miss L. is sleeping too sound to miss me.

Found Sophie Leblonk rummaging in her suitcase. She looked cross that I'd walked in on her. Slammed the lid & pushed it back under the bed. Instead of her uniform she was wearing a v. elegant purple dress. Probbly a cast-off from Lily Lopez. (If I was a real lady's maid I would get Miss Lamb's old frocks.) Sophie must be planning to meet a fellow ON THE SLY & hoped no one would see her. There's not many to choose from here: only the Footman & Sir M.'s snooty valet. Unless she's up to something more sinister! But why would she get all dressed up?

I acted all frendly & inquired about Miss Lopez & her sore throat. Sophie shrugged. 'Sore throat. ED-ache. Just an excuse she uses whenever she is bored wiz zee company. So she can go early to bed.'

Sometimes Sophie sounds so offhand when speaking about her mistress. Even tho I'm not really Miss Lamb's maid I hope I come across as Respeckful & Loyal. (Gran would be proud of me!)

Then Sophie skipped out of the room—grinning & saying 'I have zee a-pointment! Ssshh! Don't tell!!' A whiff of

Lily's perfume went with her.

I wouldn't like to be flitting about Midwinter Manor all on my own in the dark.

(What a daft thing to put—that's just what I have done!)

41 AMATEUR HOUSEMAIDING

Quentin stood outside the library. It was very late, and very dark. He'd had to wait until it was likely that everyone was in bed. That didn't mean there was *nobody* lurking about. But Nancy had ventured in here. Twice. He had to do it.

When he pushed at the door it swung inwards without a sound. All was deadly still, and deathly quiet. His torch beam swung across the floor, the walls, the shadowy alcoves. Windows looked outwards over the moat, windows looked inwards to the courtyard; and in the middle, a door that let on to the courtyard as well. *That* must have been where the mysterious figure ran from. Quentin had overheard gruff male voices. Was it one of them? Had they done the dark deed? Was that why they fled?

He inspected the door. It was locked, and there was no key. Just as Nancy reported, the room was empty of clues.

Now to find the opening to the secret passageway. Nancy had said something about it being easy to know where to look if you were a housemaid. And mentioned a single silver candlestick… There was one on the nearest mantlepiece. Was it—could it possibly be—a lever that opened the secret panel?!

He reached out to grab it, tripped over the edge of the hearth, and the torch flew out of his hand. He heard it thud against the wall panelling and crash to the floor. The noise filled the air and echoed round the room. He stood as still as a terrified mouse and waited for someone to come dashing in.

The butler waving a shotgun, or the footman with an empty sack to fling over an intruder's head.

Or a murderer returning to the scene of his crime!

Nothing happened.

Snowy silence reigned again.

Quentin tiptoed carefully across the hearthrug to retrieve his torch. It lay on the floorboards, shining brightly at the wall just inches away. At a panel beautifully carved with a pattern of leaves and, in the centre, one perfect apple.

Housemaids dusted fiddly bits of carving; somebody had to. And what had Scottie said? Look for a *roundel*. Little round pieces of carving. An apple was round. Nancy must have found it while dusting. Quentin was vague about the duties of *visiting* maidservants, but he skipped over this detail. He grasped the apple firmly and twisted it. The panel gave slightly. He was right!

Behind him a deep, disapproving voice enquired, 'What the devil are you up to? In this room, and at this hour?'

42 QUENTIN THE INVENTOR

Quentin twisted the carved apple back to its original position, and turned his body so that he was in front of it and facing his questioner. *Now* was not the moment to reveal a secret passage.

'I repeat, what are you doing in here?'

Light shone in from the half-open door. Against it, Quentin could only see that the owner of the voice was clad in black. He didn't look stout enough to be that nasty Marmaduke Roxburgh. Or tall enough to be the footman he'd seen at breakfast. So who was he?

'Must—must—have been sleepwalking,' he mumbled. Which was a brilliant idea! He made a great show of shaking the muzziness from his head and blinking his eyes.

'With a torch?'

'Yes. Terrible habit, sleepwalking.' Quentin warmed to his story. In his own way, he was good at inventing. 'They trained me to carry a torch. So I don't fall downstairs and break my neck or anything like that. While I'm wandering round. In my sleep.'

What if this *was* the murderer returning to the scene of his crime? Quentin wished he hadn't mentioned anything about breaking necks.

'That doesn't sound right to me,' the voice remarked.

Quentin babbled, playing for time. 'Oh yes, it is. Quite right. Quite right.' And then he wondered if this ridiculous tale might somehow get back to his parents, who would deny it. 'Erm, boarding school. I only do it at boarding school. They were the ones who had the torch idea. But they never told my parents. Didn't want to worry 'em. You know how it is.'

Quentin eyed the door at the far end of the room. Could he make a dash for it? Would he get there before his pursuer caught up? He began to slide away from the wall.

The voice trapped him. 'Why's that?'

'Um—it's all down to hunger. I'm a growing boy, you know. School's always stingy with food. Not like at home.' Another brilliant invention!

'Hunger?'

'Yes. See this?' Quentin reached into his dressing gown pocket, into the fluffy depths, and pulled out a hard-boiled egg. The one he'd put in there at breakfast time, just in case. He scarcely knew his own brilliance!

The man gave a disbelieving snort. 'Where did you get that?'

Quentin shrugged extravagantly and backed a few steps further away. 'No idea. Not a clue. That's what it's like when you go sleepwalking. You just never know what you've been up to, afterwards.'

A sudden shaft of light fell across the library floor— the door at the far end was opening. Could this be his chance of rescue? Or had things just got bleaker? He made out the shape of a woman, a purple dress, a look on her face that was both surprised and cross. No one he recognized.

'Better get out of here. Sharpish,' the man said. His voice was rough-edged. 'I'm meeting someone, and I don't need you hanging around.' He stepped back, holding the door open wide.

Quentin didn't wait to be told a second time. He dodged out and ran for the stairs. 'Who are you, anyway?' he demanded, once he was well out of reach.

'If you must know, I'm Mr Nash. What's your name?' Grumpily, as if he might report him.

'Scottie,' Quentin flung back over his shoulder. 'Scottie Otter.'

Q.—

There's all sorts of goings-on tonight.
Just heard rumours about another
S***** P****** in Long Gallery.

Did you find what I told you about?

N.

43 INTRUDER-ESS

NANCY'S JOURNAL

Must have fallen asleep soon as I hit the pillow. Then I woke with a start! The room was dark but I could see SOMEONE STANDING AT THE END OF MY BED. Just staring at me. It was all I could do not to scream. (Probbly did let out some sort of a <u>squeek</u>.) I clutched the blankets to my chin & just kept watching. Waiting for them to make a move. Felt like my eyes would pop out with fear.

Whoever it was just stood there—not moving—as if they were FROZEN.

There was a big lump under the covers on Sophie's bed so I knew she was back from her adventures & fast asleep. She let out a snore—& <u>still</u> the creature didn't budge.

Whoever was in our room hadn't come for her. They'd come for <u>me</u>!!

By then my eyes were used to the dark. This is what I saw: –

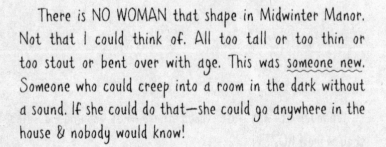

There is NO WOMAN that shape in Midwinter Manor. Not that I could think of. All too tall or too thin or too stout or bent over with age. This was <u>someone new</u>. Someone who could creep into a room in the dark without a sound. If she could do that—she could go anywhere in the house & nobody would know!

No ordinary <u>Human Being</u> could stay that still. What kind of <u>Un-Human Being</u> it could it be?!

Until it struck me! (I don't mean the intruder.) (Or Intruder-ress.)

'She' was a DRESS-FORM!! Of course she didn't move. A stuffed dummy you pin sewing on can't go anywhere. I took no notice of it in the corner when I was getting ready for bed (& busy writing my notes) & my eyes glued shut the moment the light was out.

Sophie snorted in her sleep again—like she was laughing at me.

I was stark wide awake by then & feeling v. foolish. Since there was no more sleep for me I could not help but fall to thinking. Whatever comes into your head in the DARKEST HOURS OF THE NIGHT they always seem to be the DARKEST THOGHTS & it's near impossible to get rid of them.

I tried to picture everyone safe at home in Bread Street to take my mind off it but Midwinter Manor kept getting in the way.

When the Police arrive—and they <u>will</u> arrive—they'll study the Scene of the Crime. They will look for evidence. They're bound to examine those candlesticks! I wiped the one I picked up with my hankerchief so the silver didn't spoil. But what if that didn't wipe off <u>my fingerprints??</u> Lady Sleete will tell them I was the one who found the body.

Then they'll have:-
> a Suspect
> + a Weapon
> + Evidence

The only thing they won't have is a Motive (why I did it) but <u>will that matter</u>?!

The Future looked very dark for me just then. Even tho it's daylight now I can't shake off the creepy feeling. Of someone standing over me &

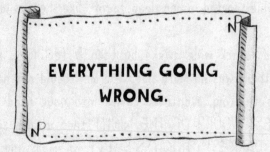

EVERYTHING GOING WRONG.

Scribbling all this down in Miss Lamb's bathroom while she's sitting up in bed with a breakfast tray. Just heard voices begin on the other side of the wall. Talking & laughing like before. Must be Miss Lopez in her room & someone else—not Sophie Leblonk. It's 2 English voices. I'm going to put this notebook down & press my ear to the wall.

(This is not being NOSY. This is being a Detective.)

44 THE FAMOUS
LILY LOPEZ

NANCY'S JOURNAL

LATER

What I heard was Lily Lopez saying 'That was over months ago, Nesta . . . (water splashing so I couldn't hear) . . . thoght you didn't care for him any more.'

So they were only talking about love affairs. I almost stopped earwigging. Then the other voice—further off & muffled—said something about a Plan.

Much nearer and clearer Lily replied 'It's plain foolish. It won't work.'

The other voice went 'All very well for you Lily . . . mumble mumble . . . some rich man will sweep you off your feet . . . mumble . . . rest of us do what we can.'

More water wooshing like someone getting out the bath & the words: 'Surely you know he's really not a nice man? I wouldn't trust him for the world.'

'I don't care . . . more mumbling . . . take my chances. You'll see.'

Next came Lily laughing & saying 'Better do your job Nesta! Hand me that towel.'

Nobody in the house called Nesta so far as I know.

Could be one of Lady Sleete's servants? When Edie Little was having that moan to me she said they helped out when lady visitors did not bring a maid. Except Lily _did_ bring one (Sophie). But a maid would never call Miss Lopez by her first name.

Miss Lamb called me back in just then. Barely touched her breakfast! She wanted something for a headache. Said 'I swear that Butler kept topping up my wine-glass. I sipped at it—out of nerves—but every time I looked it was full again. Oh heavens! Did I make a fool of myself? Lady Sleete would love that.'

So I said I'd ask Miss Lopez. (A party girl like Lily is bound to know about the Demon Drink & its effecks!) Besides it was a good excuse to nip next door. I was nearly out the room when Miss Lamb told me to take the dress she wore last night & ask Lily's maid for advice cos she'd spilled something on it. (Oh dear—if I was a real lady's maid I would have spotted that.)

Who should answer Lily's door but Sophie Leblonk!? There was a grin on her face but she quickly wiped it off when she saw me. I was polite as can be. Lily called out 'Who is it?' & then 'Send her in.'

So that's how I got to speak to the famous Miss Lily Lopez at last. She was sitting there in a long robe trimmed with white fur. Just bathed & without any make-up she looked prettier than ever.

But I messed up my chance! Every single thing I'd wanted to say flew out of my stupid head. Cos all I could think of was: she called Sophie 'Nesta'—& Sophie called her 'Lily'. Like old frends. I gawped at them & I stuttered & couldn't get anything sensible out.

Then Miss Lopez supprised me by saying 'So this is the famous Nancy Parker! So sweet—all freckles and frizz. Your mistress thinks the world of you, my dear.'

I blushed to the roots of my hair—& probbly all over my head as well. Managed to get a few words out in the end. Lily said she had a sure remedy for what she called The-Morning-After-The-Night-Before & would take it to 'poor dear Minta' herself.

'Becos darling' she explained to me 'it's <u>part of my job</u> to look as FRESH AS A DAISY at any moment. Part of my job when I am <u>invited</u> somewhere like this. In the privacy of my own home—when I wake up feeling LIKE DEATH—I'm free to look as bad as I feel! Aren't I? So-<u>phee</u>?'

She said Sophie's name like that & winked at her. (Lily has long lashes & looks very charming when she winks.) Sophie trotted off into the dressing room going 'Yes Miss Lopez. Of course Miss Lopez. I'll fetch some-zing for Mees Lamb's Ed right away.'

It was <u>far from</u> the voice I heard through the wall.

I showed Sophie the frock & asked if she knew how to get stains out of velvet. Lily was putting on her slippers

& snorted (very nicely) saying 'Good luck.' Sophie took one glance at the frock & said 'Salt.'

Lily nodded. 'I say. Well done!' & skipped off to Miss Lamb in the Rose Room—laughing as she went.

LATER STILL

Had to run downstairs for some salt & that's where I found Edie Little again. LUCKILY. Didn't know if I was to mix salt with water (hot or cold?)—or just sprinkle it dry on the velvet—& then what? There was nothing I could recall from Lady Pouncey's Book of Household Management on how to treat stains & I can't say we have much in the way of velvet at home. (Gran just boils everything to get it clean. Aunty Bee favours dabbing with a drop of clear vinegar.) Plus it was really Miss Beaumont's frock. I couldn't let it go back to her all spoiled.

'Salt! WHAT? Never!!' Edie shreeked. Then she looked at me kindly saying I was very young for a Lady's Maid so I confessed to being new to the job. I was just following advice from Miss Lopez's maid & she must be used to taking care of frocks if anyone was.

'Is that how they do it in France?' Edie said shaking her head in despair. Salt would only harm—not help—& that daft girl was talking out of her hat. If I took her the frock she would see what she could do.

I left feeling most GRATEFUL towards Edie Little—&
most annoyed towards Sophie Leblonk. So—I shall write
down my new suspishuns if I get time.

45 NOT WHAT SHE SEEMS

NANCY'S JOURNAL

Sophie Leblonk is not at all what she seems! Here's my evidence:-

* She's not a real Lady's Maid. The salt—& Lily laughing & saying 'Good luck' & 'Well done'—like Sophie was just ~~ges~~ guessing. I bet she knows NO MORE than I do.
* In private she acts like a frend not a maid. Judging on what I overheard thru the wall—twice!
* Yet talking to me she sounded Spiteful & Jellous of Lily.
* Is 'Sophie Leblonk' a made-up name? Lily called her Nesta.
* Is she truly French? Seems she just puts on that voice when it suits. NOTE: ask Miss Lamb if that's how a real French person sounds. (I'm sure she knows.)
* She has sneaky habits & she's nosy with it.
* Doesn't like me being nosy back. Very careful about her suitcase.
* What was she up to last night? All dressed up & nowhere to go! Who was she meeting?
* Was it the Mystery Man Lily said she does not trust? Could it be that slimy valet Nash? I saw them nattering away at Servants Breakfast like they knew

each other. Is it really a Love Affair or something darker?

* Cos what did she mean by A Plan?
* Big ??? What was she up to on the night that Osmond Phipps met his death? Didn't see her at all after Servants Supper. I spent all night on Miss Lamb's couch. So there is NO EVIDENCE of where she was.

Now my Theory is that Sophie is an IMPOSTER! And Lily Lopez is in on the trick!!

Sophie was already on my list of Possible Murderers. Now she's No. 1! With Lily as her ackumpliss. Or is Lily the one in charge with Sophie following orders? Did Osmond Phipps dig up the dirt on Lily Lopez? Something so bad that they would murder to cover it up! Was Lady Sleete going to BLACKMAIL her?! And what does the Mystery Man know about it?

Which reminds me—Sophie never seemed worried or downcast about a death in the house. In fact she was downright cheerful about it. No wunder!

SECRET FILE

ON

LILY LOPEZ

Where are these now??!

If this can be proved then I'm in the clear.

Trouble is—I'm on <u>shaky ground</u> here. Cos I am AN IMPOSTER OF SORTS & Miss Lamb is in on our trick. And <u>we</u> are not up to anything wicked.

46 BREAKFAST WITH A PRINCESS

Learning from yesterday's mistake, Quentin went down early for breakfast. It seemed that everyone else was late. There was nobody there but the tiny old lady with the ear trumpet—Princess Canova—and the footman waiting on her. Quentin loaded his plate with more than enough of everything from the sideboard and sat down near, but not too near, the Princess.

'I know you,' she said in her cracked and creaky voice. 'You're the Otter boy.'

He knew who she was now, but he didn't know how to address her. Was it 'Your Highness', or just 'Ma'am'? In the end he mumbled something between the two. 'No, Mmmnnhhss, I'm Quentin Ives.' She frowned back at him, disbelieving. Or not hearing properly.

They ate in silence for a while, until the Princess said, 'I hear he's invented a new kind of wheel.'

'Who has, Hmmmnnss?'

'So clever.'

Quentin was fairly clear in his mind that the wheel was invented thousands upon thousands of years ago and that was pretty much it. Round. With a hole in the middle. Hard to improve upon.

'A new motor car wheel. So that the vehicle doesn't slide all over the road. In bad weather. Or on steep hills.'

Quentin thought about the drive to Midwinter, and feeling more and more sick as the car slithered about. A new kind of wheel could only be a good thing. Though she probably meant a new kind of motor-tyre.

'Such a clever man, your father,' Princess Canova said. Quentin looked up and found her bright beady eyes on him. So he nodded.

The footman came in with a steaming kipper under a silver lid which he presented to the old lady with great ceremony. The smell of it wafted across to Quentin. He realized that he had stuffed down too much food, too quickly; also that he'd never liked kippers.

The Princess raised her fork with a sliver of fish hanging from it. 'Do have one if you want. You've only to tell the footman and he'll fetch one for you. Two, if you'd like. I know how you growing boys like to eat.'

Feeling queasy, Quentin just smiled and said nothing. The smell of the kipper and the memory of the car ride were overlapping now. And the memory of his alarming encounter last night.

'That chap—you know the one—' the old lady continued, '*his* name was Fish.'

Quentin said nothing.

'Osborne Fish. Peculiar name. Jasper Grant recommended him to her Ladyship. Heaven knows what for.'

Quentin glanced at the footman who stood beside

the door like a statue, his face a blank mask. When he looked back the old lady's mischievous eyes were still on him. She lowered her creak to a croak and whispered, 'The chap in the library, that's who I mean…'

Quentin thought he might actually be sick if he didn't get out of the room right away. He grabbed two pieces of dry toast and shoved them into his dressing gown pocket. 'Must dash,' he said, 'Your Mnnnhhsss. Bye.'

47 MIXED UP

'No, I haven't overheard any more *juicy snippets*, Quentin. You make me sound like the most frightful gossip.'

His mother sat in front of the mirror, putting on her earrings. In the dressing room his father was shaving. Through the open door Quentin could hear him humming, whistling, and occasionally harrumphing.

'I didn't mean that,' Quentin insisted. 'It's just that, like you said, there's some very *interesting* guests here and I'm trying to take—um—an *interest*. Like Mr Jasper Grant, fr'instance.'

Mrs Ives sighed. 'And some of them are very tedious. I was next to Mr Hawk at dinner and he must be the dullest man on earth. What was he droning on about? Oh, yes, he was under the strange delusion that your father hopes to build a motor racing track on an aeroplane landing strip left over from the War. Then on the other side I had Princess Canova, and it's impossible to get a sensible conversation out of her.'

Mr Ives stuck his head around the door, his jaw half-covered in white lather. 'Landing strip? You know that Godfrey owns an old landing strip? Though Lord knows what he proposes to do with it.'

'Does he? Lucky Godfrey!' Mrs Ives snorted. She banged face powder onto her nose. Quentin knew that talk of his Uncle Godfrey always made her cross. His father's younger brother had done very well for himself out of the War, and although Mummy disapproved, she was also frightfully envious.

'Never heard he was interested in motor racing, though,' mumbled Mr Ives, going back to his shaving.

'Geoffrey?' Quentin's mother paused, powder puff in mid-air. 'You don't think that they could possibly have got us *mixed up*, do you?'

His father put his head round the door again. 'Mixed up with what?'

'Mixed up with your brother. With Godfrey Ives. When they invited us.'

Quentin's father did a lot of noisy harrumphing which ended with him saying, 'No, of course not. Not possible. No.'

'Only,' his mother went on, 'you don't have acres and acres of land, or an airstrip, or a mad plan about motor racing, and Mr Hawk was convinced that you did.'

'Yes,' said Quentin, 'and when I ran into Mr Grant, he seemed to think I was the son of *Godfrey* Ives.'

'What?!'

'I'm only saying, that's what he said…' He remembered the peculiar aeroplane impression, too.

Mrs Ives slammed her powder puff back into its box and crushed the lid on, raising a small cloud of pink dust around it. She glared at her own reflection in the mirror, then noticed Quentin, behind her.

'Quentin! Get out of that wretched dressing gown

before you do anything else. I want to see you looking presentable when you come downstairs later.'

'Come downstairs…?'

'For the charades. Have you forgotten already?'

'Oh,' said Quentin. His insides felt funny again.

'Put on your smart jacket.'

'Mmmm?' said Quentin.

'The tartan one you like to wear for parties.'

'Ah. Just remembered. I promised Miss Kettle I'd…' Quentin didn't bother to finish his sentence, and scuttled out of the door.

48 INCHING NEARER THE TRUTH

NANCY'S JOURNAL

Just had 3 v. useful encounters!

1st Edie Little

Took Miss Lamb's frock back down to Edie Little where she helped me get it clean. In the Laundry Room—with just the 2 of us—she began moaning again. About how Lady Sleete cuts corners. 'But only with us servants. THEM UPSTAIRS must never feel the pinch—oh no! She has us work til we drop so they don't have to lift a hand.' I kept quiet & let her grumble on becos:

**A Good Detective is a Good Listener!
You never know what someone may let slip.**

I found out where the Cript is!!

Edie said 'Leastways no one has to go & fetch the ice from the Ice House in this weather. They just chop it out of the yard.' I never head of an Ice House before. Edie was supprised at my Ignorance & asked if Miss Lamb's family did not have such a thing. That's when I remembered that I was supposed to work for Miss Lamb all the time! Thank goodness I wasn't so TAKEN OFF GARD that I blurted out she just lived in a 3-room flat. Instead I told Edie that 'her London household was not quite as grand as Midwinter Manor'!! Made it sound like Miss L. might have any number of houses elsewhere.

Turns out you need ice all year round for fancy puddings & drinks & what-not. That's where an Ice House comes in handy. It's buried in the hill above the Manor. Edie says the servants go out thru a tunnel under the moat that you get to from the Cript—so they don't use the main door & the bridge. In olden days the Sleete family were very church-y & had a Chapel inside the walls of Midwinter Manor with a Cript below it. Now the Cript is a storeroom & the Chapel turned into bedrooms.

I meant to ask Edie if she'd ever met Sophie Leblonk before—& Nash the Valet. But another servant came in & she got in a right old panic about how much time she'd wasted chatting & sent me packing.

2nd Sophie Leblonk (!)

On my way back I overheard voices in the Servants Hall. It was Sophie & Nash HAVING WORDS! The door was a crack open & I tucked myself in the dark passageway where they wouldn't see me. Nash was his usual slimy self. But Sophie sounded angry. She quite forgot her Frenchified way of speaking. (More evidence!) Seems she'd hoped to meet Marmaduke Roxber last night but Nash came instead. She demanded to speak to Sir M.—and soon. Nash said he could not just tell his master what to do. Sophie replied that she was sure he had his ways & it would be IN HIS INTERESTS to help her. The next words chilled my blood. Nash said 'Oh you'll get him by hook or by crook will you? Is it BLACKMAIL now?'

Sophie came bursting out the door (nearly knocked me over) & stamped off.

That's why she was dressed up last night. She expected to meet Sir M. & it didn't sound like a Love Affair to me.

3rd Miss Beans Otter

A girl came dashing down the stairs as I went up & tripped over her own feet. She had a big book in her arms & scraps of paper flew out all over the place. I helped her gather them up. Must say she has good manners—she said Thank-You very nicely & inter-duced herself. I admired her book & she told me it was her Dad's idea for her to keep a Scrapbook on their travels.

'I cut things out of the papers—any snippet I liked the look of. Kings & Queens. Racing Drivers. Bally dancers.

But the glue doesn't always stick very well.' I glanced at the scrap still in my hand: 2 pretty ladies smiling for the camera. I said 'That's Lily Lopez. You know she's staying here don't you Miss?' She said yes & that she had a <u>whole page</u> of Lily Lopez as her picture was always in the British papers.

I saw the lines written under the picture & had a shock. I looked at the picture again—carefully. I am going to stick it in here cos Miss Beans Otter said I could keep it.

Miss Lily Lopez and Miss Nesta Vye enjoying the sunshine. Miss Lopez is currently starring in the musical comedy 'Summer Frolics' at the Duke's Theatre, where Miss Vye is her understudy.

And Lo & behold—who does Nesta Vye look like? Sophie Leblonk that's who!!

<u>Understudy</u> means someone who learns your part in a play & goes on if you are IN-DISPOSED. (Tho we never had understudies at Sunday School. We just had to get on with it. Wally Green played King Herod with a stinking cold & no one could understand a word he said.) So Nesta is really an actress just like Lily. But not nearly so famous or sucksessful. Explains <u>a lot</u>:—

- why she is jellous
- how she can make everyone think she's French
- why she & Lily are such chums in private
- why she's no more a Ladies Maid than I am!

I'm inching nearer The Truth. <u>Sophie</u> is blackmailing <u>Marmaduke Roxber</u>. With evidence <u>she stole</u> off Osmond Phipps. That's why she wants to see him in such a flaming hurry. And that's what she meant by her Plan!

49 THE LONG GALLERY

Miss Kettle waited by the narrow staircase which led to the top floor of the West Range.

'Quentin. Berenice. No Prescott?'

Beans shook her head. 'Dad's got him helping tidy up his paperwork. Scottie loves that, it makes him feel grown-up. He said he's tired of *playing with the children!*'

'Well, thank you two for coming along.' Miss Kettle was holding a black-and-white dog which she unloaded into Quentin's arms. 'This is Lady Sleete's spaniel, Plum. I'm sure he will enjoy your company. You may notice that he's rather stout and rather spoilt. Plum isn't fond of steps, especially steep ones, but once you reach the Long Gallery he *must* walk. No fewer than six times up and down, please, children. Then you may deliver him back to Her Ladyship's rooms.'

When she had gone, Quentin peered up the creaky-looking stairs. Plum was very heavy. 'You first,' he said to Beans.

The Long Gallery ran the whole length of the west side of Midwinter Manor. It was made for exercise, not for sitting about. The few chairs were hard and straight-backed, the tables only big enough to display a bowl or a vase. Gloomy old paintings lined the walls. There was a single, empty, fireplace that looked as if it hadn't seen a fire in years. A row of small windows faced out over the moat, towards a cluster of bleak outbuildings and several motor cars almost buried in snow.

According to Nancy, somewhere in here was the entrance to another secret passage. Another way of listening in to your enemies! Quentin looked about for roundels or roses or apples, but the panelling here was much plainer, carved in lines, and only reached halfway up the walls. The ceiling curved like the inside of a boat. How could a passageway be hidden anywhere here? It didn't look promising. Besides, he still had his commission to carry out for Lamb-and-Mint-Sauce. That was an actual 'case' to follow up; this was merely a rumour.

'Um, Beans,' he began, 'd'you mind doing this by yourself? Only I've got some rather important business of my own.'

'*What* important business?'

'I've been asked to apply my powers of observation to, well, to our hostess. To Lady Sleete.' He just mouthed the last two words, as if someone might be listening.

'Who asked? Why?'

Quentin puffed out his chest. ''Fraid I can't give away details.'

'Don't go, Quentin. It's so cold and dreary up here. It will be miserable on my own.'

'Any news on the stolen papers yet?'

'Not as far as I know. Dad is keeping very quiet about it.'

'Bad luck. But I can't stay. It's rather urgent.' Urgent because he didn't get anywhere yesterday.

Beans added, 'Miss Kettle seemed to say that Lady Sleete will be keeping to her rooms this morning. So you won't see her anyway, not unless you come with me to take Plum back.'

Quentin grunted, then realized that he sounded just like his father. He tried to turn the grunt into a considered 'Hmmm'. Beans took this for agreement. 'Oh thank you, Quent. You're a good friend.'

Quent, indeed!

They walked on, while Plum sniffed at the rugs and the legs of chairs and cabinets. Quentin couldn't resist saying, 'By the way, I found the other end of that passage last night.'

'*What?*' Beans stopped abruptly and he bumped into her. Plum stopped too, snuffled up something from the floor, and ate it.

'It's true.' Quentin glanced around and shivered. The eyes of twenty or more Sleete ancestors stared down at them. He whispered, 'It *does* come out in the library. Beside the fireplace at the East end. There's a carved apple that opens it.'

Beans didn't keep her voice down. 'Great news! How did you discover that?'

Quentin decided to ignore this question. 'Also, I'm informed there may be another,'—he mouthed the words *secret passage*,—'up here.'

'Who told you?'

'Just say, *a friend*.'

'The same one who's asked you to spy on—?'

'Sshh.'

'Well, then. No time to lose. You take that end, I'll take this one.'

She ran off to look behind a large tapestry that hung on the far wall. Quentin turned in the opposite direction. Plum lay down and watched with polite interest as they worked their way up and down, then down and up.

'Nothing,' said Beans, dusting her hands on the back of her skirt. 'Nothing,' Quentin agreed. 'My informant may have been mistaken.'

Just as he was saying that, Beans let out a sharp cry. 'It's an S-shape that's carved into the panels, isn't it?'

'Ye-e-s,' said Quentin, who hadn't actually noticed until now.

'S for Sleete.'

Quentin squinted at the walls. Every panel had an S inscribed in its lines, zigzagging across. Now that Beans had pointed it out, the shape jumped out at him.

'But look at this!' She stood beneath a painting of a man on a horse. There was a snake on the ground between its hooves. Neither horse nor rider looked particularly alarmed. 'Look at the snake.'

Quentin looked. The snake was brown. The horse was black. There was nothing remarkable to see at all.

'See the shape of it, and the way it's pointing!'

The snake was like an S in reverse, its head down, and its darting tongue pointing to the top of the S in the panel below.

Beans crowed, 'It's telling us that *this* is the place!'

Quentin stepped towards the wall, pushing up his dressing gown sleeves in readiness. He was the expert here, after all. 'There's no roundel, or Tudor rose, or apple. Nothing to push or twist.'

By now Beans was jumping up and down. 'Do

something else, then.'

Quentin placed his fingertips on the diagonal of the S. It was slightly raised. He pulled. Nothing. He turned the other way and pulled. Nothing.

Beans elbowed him out of the way, fitted her smaller hands round the top of the S and pressed. Still nothing. She worked her fingertips carefully along. With a sudden clatter the panel fell out on to the floor. Ancient dust flew with it.

Plum gave one short bark. A dark rectangular hole gaped in front of them. Beans peered inside. 'Looks like steps straight down. As far as I can make out.'

'We haven't brought a torch,' said Quentin.

Beans pulled a box of safety matches out of her skirt pocket. 'Dad taught me always to be practical. Now, who's going in?'

'We both are. Aren't we?'

Plum put his head down and barked again, right into the hole. Beans said, 'One of us should stay with the dog. Stop him diving down there and barking his head off. Giving the game away.'

'Where do the steps lead?' Quentin glanced about, trying to gauge matters. 'Let me see, which end is this…?'

'The *South* end of the *West* Range, of course. Right below us are Lady Sleete's rooms!'

'Then I'll go,' Quentin said, drawing a deep breath. 'It must be me.' He shrugged off his bulky dressing gown.

'Good-oh,' agreed Beans, in a manner far too jolly for his liking.

Heart quaking, Quentin dropped into the dark gaping maw.

50 IN THE GAPING MAW

'Shoes,' Beans reminded him, and Quentin stopped, drawing his feet up again. He toed off one shoe, then the other, and began again.

'Don't forget your matches!' Beans struck the first one for him. 'Best of luck, Quent!'

By wavering match-light he crept down the first few stairs. The flame burnt down and licked at his fingers, then went out.

'Here, I found this,' hissed a voice above him, and a hand reached down with a candle in it. 'Wait!'

He waited. The next thing Beans handed him was a warm sock.

'Wrap that over your hand to protect it from the melting wax.'

Beans had indeed been raised to be practical.

His did as she said, but then didn't have enough hands to light the candle! In the end he sat down, wedging the candle between his knees while he struck a match. The inside of the secret passage sprang to life around him. He mustn't think about cobwebs, or spiders, or deathwatch beetles gnawing through the wood. Or how narrow the space was. Or how fiercely his heart was thumping, as if it might burst out of his chest. He just wouldn't let those thoughts into his mind *at all*. He looked at Beans's fawn sock, which was strangely comforting. Step by step, he descended into the flickering dark.

The staircase twisted, echoing the one that had led up to the Long Gallery. He could just about see where it ended when suddenly a voice at his shoulder said, 'Araminta Lamb!'

Quentin jumped. He almost dropped the candle.

The voice was right beside him. But there was no one in the passageway. There was no room for anyone but him.

'If it wasn't for her, I wouldn't be in this fix at all!'

The woman's voice was sharp and impatient. The sort that could penetrate through walls. Quentin realized that whoever was speaking must be close by on the other side, with just a carved wooden panel between them. He crouched as still as a statue, barely breathing, in case she heard him. Hot candle wax began to roll down on to the sock stretched over his hand.

A man's voice, more distant, replied, 'It seems to me that you've brought this fix on yourself. And trying to hush it up is plain wrong.'

'I wouldn't call it *hushing up*, Jasper.' So that's who it was. The other voice was Lady Sleete, of course. She went on, 'It's simply better that people know as little as possible.'

Jasper Grant said, 'You won't stop them wondering.'

'There is nothing to wonder *about*. I've made the whole business sound as dull as can be.'

'It's still a very bad business.'

Quentin wondered if they meant the murder, or the theft, or both.

Lady Sleete's voice came again, icy and very near. 'I know people talk. As for the servants they bring—unlike mine, they're not to be trusted an inch! If only Lily Lopez hadn't come. Theatre types are such gossips, and what they don't know for sure, they'll invent.'

'*You* invited her, Margery.'

'Because Lily is such a draw. Having her here meant that Marmaduke Roxburgh would say yes to my invitation.'

'Bees to the honeypot.'

Lady Sleete gave something like a growl. 'I instructed that man Phipps to send me his report in good time. Instead he was late and came in person, demanding to see me. So inconvenient of him.'

'So inconvenient that now he's *dead*.'

Quentin shivered at the word.

'That's not what I meant,' snapped Lady Sleete. 'It was almost dinner time when he arrived and I had to be with my guests. So I told Henry Hawk to meet him. Phipps was alive and well when Henry left him.'

'But neither alive nor well now.' Jasper Grant's voice grew louder and quieter as if he was pacing up and down. 'I wish I'd never given you his card in the first place.'

Quentin's left foot was tingling with pins and needles. But he couldn't move. He must hear as much as possible—for Miss Lamb's sake. And for Nancy's. She had the detective's actual card saved in her notebook. This was absolute gold dust!

Lady Sleete spoke sharply. 'If only James had fallen for a suitable girl! *That's* what started all the bother.'

'Someone like Pansy Roxburgh, you mean? You did mention her name rather a lot last night.'

'There'd be no need for me to look into Pansy Roxburgh's background. But this Lamb woman! Lord knows who she is. Though I know what she's after—the family name! James is the Sleete heir.' She gave a harsh laugh. 'I don't suppose she knows there's barely any money left.'

'It couldn't possibly be the case that she and James are in love?'

'Really, Jasper. This isn't one of your books.'

'No. I don't write murder mysteries.'

Quentin shivered again. The candle flame shook.

Lady Sleete went on, almost in his ear, 'Everything's such a mess, and after all my hard work! Finding a funny little American for Marmaduke to invest in. And that Ives chap with a race track that would make a perfect gift for Pansy. But if I can keep everyone calm my planning may just pay off…'

'Are you saying everything was a ruse to matchmake the Sleetes with the Roxburghs?'

'Don't look so astonished, Jasper. It's how marriages—and fortunes—have always been made.'

Quentin's brain was a-whirl with information. The candle was dripping wax all over Beans's sock and the heat of it burned through to his skin. He would have to move before he set the whole place on fire.

Lady Sleete's voice had moved away and he could hardly make out the words. Perhaps they had their heads together, plotting. Time to climb out of the maw. He stood up. Hot wax flooded the candle flame and he found himself in sudden darkness, surrounded by the reek of waxy smoke.

'Can you smell something?' came that piercing voice again. 'Just like—I don't know—singeing socks. How extremely odd.'

51 TEAMS

''Fraid it's a bit . . . ' Quentin handed Beans her ruined sock. He felt proud of himself. His knees were still shaking, but he had done it. No panicking, no running away. And Beans was there to witness it, and say *Well done*. Except that what she actually said was, 'Well?'

Quentin rolled his eyes. 'You were right when you said secret passages were a good way of listening in on your enemies!'

'Tell me everything.'

But he couldn't. He had to find Miss Lamb—and Nancy Parker. 'Later. Promise. But I've got to go. You'll have to take Plum back to Lady Sleete yourself.'

Beans looked down at her legs, one in a long fawn sock, the other bare. 'Do you think she'll notice?'

'I can assure you she's got other things on her mind right now. By the way, d'you know if your father is going into business with Marmaduke Roxburgh? That's what Lady Sleete is aiming for.'

'That snake? No! I expect he's the one who stole Dad's papers. I wouldn't put it past him.'

'I've been thinking that, too.'

'Really, Quent? Have you?'

'Roxburgh probably gave the instructions. He's got a very sly-looking valet. I'm sure *he'd* do it.'

'Why hasn't Lady Sleete ordered everyone's rooms to be searched?'

'She won't want to upset her guests, and she'll swear that her own servants are utterly trustworthy. That's what she said just now. She and Jasper Grant were talking about hushing up this whole bad business.'

'You *can't* go without telling me more!' cried Beans, jumping up and down and waking Plum, who was stretched out on the floor. 'Quentin, you're a selfish pig! You're as bad as my brother!'

But Quentin had already gone.

Within the twists and turns of Midwinter Manor it was always hard to find the person he was looking for, but horribly easy to run into those he was trying to avoid. When he turned right he saw Miss Kettle in the distance. So he swerved left, and there was his mother.

'Quentin! Dressing gown!'

He shrugged off the garment, bundled it up and stuck it under his arm. He was still wearing several layers of lumpy jumper. Mrs Ives ignored them. Her eyes sparkled.

'So exciting! Lady Sleete has asked me to organize the charades.'

'What? When? Just now?'

'In fact she asked Miss Kettle to ask me. I'm told that Her Ladyship is rather occupied this morning.'

*Pre*occupied, I'd say, thought Quentin. And wait till Mummy hears that their invitation really was intended for Uncle *Godfrey* Ives! Actually—better that she never hears that.

His mother was still gabbling on. 'It's such an honour. The charades are a great Midwinter tradition. Guests form into teams and act out well-known words or phrases for everyone to guess. I'm told that the dressing-up costumes here are marvellous, and we have a real live actress in our midst! And *I* am to choose the teams!' She glanced about anxiously. 'Though it's been hard to pin everyone down... But I'm putting your father and Mr Roxburgh together. They've become such firm friends. I shall be with Mr Grant and the little Otter girl. I'm sure she's a dear. Now, who else?' She consulted a handful of notes covered with scribbles and crossings-out. 'Ah, Mr Hawk... Well, that can't be helped.'

Quentin shuffled his feet, desperate to get away.

'Now, I've written down instructions for you here, Quentin, as I know you are such an addle-brain you'll forget.'

She handed him a sheet of Midwinter Manor notepaper. It said:

Mr Otter
Miss Lopez
Princes Canova
Quentin
Meet Oriel Room. 4 o'clock

He folded it up into a small square, which made him think of Nancy Parker. He needed to get a note to her.

'Course I won't forget,' he mumbled, and started away.

'Tartan jacket!' his mother snapped. 'You won't forget that either, will you?'

52 SOPHIE'S SUITCASE

NANCY'S JOURNAL

Got to find out what Sophie Leblonk—or rather Nesta Vye—is up to! There's something important in that suitcase under her bed & I mean to find out what! Now I think back she was always so keen to hide it. Is it she planning to BLACKMAIL Marmaduke Roxber? What has she got on him? Is it those papers Roxber grilled me about?

LATER

Looked in the suitcase. Under some very nice clothes & under-garments all in bit of a heap (& far too good for a maidservant) I did find some papers! Nothing to do with digging up dirt on a famous person. Just pages of scrawly handwriting & lots of numbers with sketches & arrows. Cannot make head nor tail of them.

Now I wunder if these are <u>Mr Otter's papers?</u> The ones they suspected Quentin of stealing. I can't take them all in case she comes back & finds them gone. So I'm taking just 1 page. I've tucked the clothes over the top & pushed it back under her bed as if nothing was up. I'm off to show the page to Quentin cos he told me about it in the 1st place. Or Miss Lamb cos she is clever. Or if I can't find them—to Mr Otter himself—as I know his room is above the Libary.

A sneaky job well done—I hope!

53 ALL GONE WRONG!

NANCY'S JOURNAL

It has all gone wrong! I'm in Miss Kettle's Eyrie. The door is locked. I am in SO MUCH TROUBLE now.

(Writing this with a pencil stub I found on Miss Kettle's mantelpiece.)

Before I found anyone to show the paper the Butler stopped me! Something about the Police. So I asked (polite as can be) if the telephone lines were fixed. He said No. But—as soon as a path was cut thru the snow—the Police would be here & it's me they'd want to speak to first. Then he spotted the page I was holding. Stuck his hand out & demanded to see what it was. So I had NO CHOICE but to give it to him.

I explained (even more polite) that it might be part of Mr Otter's missing papers & I knew where the rest of them were. I was taking it to show Mr Otter now.

'Missing Papers?!' He nearly exploded. 'What the devil do you know about Missing Papers??? Last day or two—whenever there's trouble—who do we find? You, Parker. YOU!'

He dragged me off to the Butler's Pantry. A gaggle of servants stared at us. He shoved me inside & shut the door. After an age I heard voices outside. The Butler, Miss Kettle & a nasty tone that I knew was Lawyer Hawk.

Deciding what to do with me! Mr Hawk wanted to take over. But Miss Kettle (good for her) said if there was any searching of Female Staff bedrooms to be done—then that was her job. Mr Hawk spat out in the meanest croak 'Do it then! Right away!! Make sure you report back to me.'

The door banged open & they hauled me out. Before I could explain anything I was marched off upstairs. Felt WORRIED—but not really SCARED—cos I knew they would find I was Telling the Truth. The rest of the papers were in Sophie's suitcase under her bed.

I like Miss Kettle & thoght she would be fair & hear me out. But she just stood by with a pursed mouth while the Butler asked which was my bed. Then he pulled out my case & flung it open. Still I was not VERY SCARED.

Till I saw the papers were there!!! Right on top of my spare nightgown.

'That's not right. That can't be.' I gasped—or something very like it. 'Look in Sophie's case. That's where they were not half an hour ago.'

He took her case out & opened it. Sophie's things were folded neat & tidy (not like before!) and of course nothing suspishus there at all.

'NO!' I cried. 'It's a trick!'

The Butler was furious but Miss Kettle said as I was a 'Visiting Maid' she would deal with me—& that's how I ended up in here.

But it's still BAD. She must have gone to report to Lawyer Hawk. Seems like I've been here for ages & <u>the longer I wait the worse it gets.</u>

How did Sophie switch the papers just in time? I tried to picture those faces staring at me as I vanished inside the Butler's Pantry. I swear she was there at the back of the crowd. I can see the dimple that comes when she's smiling. She knew what I'd found. Now she's put the blame on <u>me</u>!

54 CAMOMILE TEA

NANCY'S JOURNAL

I heard a key in the door & got ready to FACE MY FATE.
But it was only Edie Little sent to make me a cup of
Camomile Tea. Very soothing to the nerves she said &
poked about in a cupboard looking for the right tin. As
she put the water on to boil she told me how Miss Kettle
cooks up remedies from all kinds of herbs from the garden
to cure everyone's ills. Lady Sleete in particular relies on
them. Specially the Horehound Throat Sweets—tho Edie
said they can be hard as bullets!

I said how kind Miss Kettle was. (Mr Hawk would not
order soothing tea. He'd be pulling my fingernails out to
get me to Confess!)

'She's the only one I'll miss when I—' Edie said & then
stopped like she'd bit off her ~~tung~~ tongue.

'When I leave' was what she meant. I knew it & she knew
it. We looked at each other—sort of sizing one another
up. I was going say 'You can tell me' when she said 'I can
tell you—I'm longing to tell someone—& you'll soon be gone.'

(She did not say WHERE I'D BE GONE TO & I did not
care to dwell on it just then.)

She told me in Strick Confidence that they'd been
planning & saving for years & years—her & Betts. That's

Lady Sleete's driver. He lives over the garage & takes most of his meals out there. That's how they managed to meet in secret. They hoped to leave in the spring. As a Married Couple!

'We aim to run a little Sweetshop & live in rooms above.' She smiled as if she was looking into her dreams. Then her face clouded over. 'Her Ladyship will be so angry when she finds out. Hates her staff carrying on together—or indeed with anyone from outside—& to think it's happened behind her back!'

I swore I'd never SAY A WORD. She could trust me. Then the kettle boiled. I told Edie to take a cup of tea for her nerves too! She looked bit shocked that I should even sergest it.

CALMING CAMOMILE TEA

The tea must have calmed me a bit—for I decided to investigate further since I had Edie on my side. Wanted to know who usually opened the door to visitors. Cos I was thinking that nobody seemed to have let poor Osmond Phipps in the night he arrived. I knew it would be the Footman's job with the Butler greeting important visitors inside. But if they are both busy? Edie said it falls to one of the housemaids. (I knew that too.) But then she went on 'Or Betts if he's around. Like the other night when the station taxi dropped a gentleman off in the snow.'

That's when I found Camomile Tea does not always settle the nerves. Cos mine started jumping up & down again. But I acted Cool as a Cucumber & said 'Oh . . . Betts would let him in . . . mmm . . . I see.'

Edie glanced about as if WALLS HAD EARS then— since I was her new frend—whispered 'The poor gent who came to greef in the libary!'

I asked if Betts knew who it was & she replied 'A Mr Phipps who said he had to see Her Ladyship. Urgent. But in the end Mr Hawk—scarcely out of his overcoat—went in instead.'

Did she or Betts know what it was about? Again Edie looked a bit shifty. Then (whispering again) said that Betts was v. curious. For why would a man come in such bad weather that the taxi wouldn't wait? Perhaps he was another late guest. An UNEXPECTED one. So Betts hung about outside—until the cold got the better of him. Heard Mr Hawk & the gentleman <u>having words</u>.

At this point I was almost dancing on the hearthrug I was so im-pahsunt. I asked were they ANGRY words?

According to Edie—yes! Something about an investigation Lady Sleete had instructed him to do. Into <u>a certain lady</u>. (Not Marmaduke Roxber then! My theory dashed.) Then she got all tongue-tied & wouldn't say any more. I felt she probbly could—but my mind was running ahead. Must speak to Betts next. (Quite forgot I was <u>Imprisoned</u> at this point!)

Just one thing I had to know—the lady's name! Betting it was Lily Lopez.

'Your lady' Edie Little muttered.

My lady? I thoght she was getting me muddled up with Sophie Leblonk.

'Your lady. Staying in the Rose Room. Miss Araminta Lamb.'

55 QUENTIN'S WORD

Miss Lamb had vanished. Worryingly, so had Nancy. So he went to see Beans. He owed her an explanation. She was in her father's room, sticking news clippings in a scrapbook. Mr Otter's desk was now scrupulously tidy, with no papers in sight. Mr Otter himself was playing chess with Scottie by the fire. They had matching expressions of concentration on their faces and didn't even glance up. It was so quiet that Quentin could hear Beans scissoring through another page.

He signalled for her to slip outside so that they could talk in private but she didn't seem to—or simply refused to—understand. So he sat down at the table, pulled a magazine off the stack in front of Beans and flicked through it. What did she see in all this stuff? Pictures of people at parties. Pictures of people at a horse race. Pictures—actually the next article was about aeroplanes, and looked more interesting. He stopped flicking and concentrated.

Beans couldn't help but be curious. She leaned towards him. 'Anything worth keeping?'

Quentin pored over the details of a new biplane. Beans tapped her finger on the caption under a photograph.

'Look who it is!'

Standing beside the plane was a figure in baggy flying overalls, a leather helmet and goggles. A scarf hid the lower part of their face. It was impossible to tell who was underneath.

Beans read out loud, "*Intrepid Miss Pansy Roxburgh is best known for her success at motor racing. But last month she celebrated her twenty-first birthday by taking to the skies in her new Scout Experimental 5a, a surprise gift from her father.*"

'You know who her father is?' Quentin whispered, so low that only Beans would hear. 'Marmaduke Roxburgh, marble thief! Did you ask about him and *your* father doing business together?'

Beans rolled her eyes. 'Marmaduke Roxburgh's certainly shown a keen interest in Dad's new motor car tyre. Hasn't he, Dad?' she said loudly.

'Was that the *secret invention?*' Quentin hissed. 'The one in the *stolen papers?*'

'Oh, no. Everyone here seems to know about that.'

Even the deaf old Princess, Quentin remembered.

Beans went on, 'The latest secret's something quite different.'

Mr Otter lifted his head from the chessboard. 'Roxburgh's been trying to persuade me that the tyres should be manufactured here. I'm sure that's why Lady Sleete invited us, so that he'd have plenty of time to work on me. He'd like to buy the design and set up a factory.'

'So that he gets all the profit from your invention!' Beans added.

Mr Otter gave them both a serious look. 'I hope you're not still trying to be detectives.'

Quentin muttered to Beans, 'Why can't you set up your own factory? I thought you American Otters were millionaires?'

'Oh, people always think that. But it's the Chicago Otters, the ones who built railroads. *They're* the ones worth a fortune. We're just the ones with the crazy inventor father who—'

They were interrupted by a tap on the door. Miss Kettle came in.

'Oh, no,' Beans murmured. 'It'll be about the charades. Do we *have* to go?'

But to Quentin's detective's eye, Miss Kettle looked far too uneasy for it to be about charades. Hair was escaping from her bun and her long knitted cardigan had got twisted round her. She went straight over to Mr Otter. Without a word she stuck some papers under his nose.

Mr Otter adjusted his spectacles and gave a grunt of surprise. 'Where did you find these, Miss Kettle?'

'One of the visiting maids had them in her possession. Miss Lamb's maid, to be precise.'

Now it was Quentin's turn to grunt in surprise. Though his grunt was more like a squeak.

Mr Otter flicked through the pages he held. 'I'm very pleased to see them again, I must say. But Miss Lamb? The schoolteacher? Why in heaven . . . ?'

'We don't know if Miss Lamb has anything to do with this, but her maidservant Nancy Parker—'

Quentin couldn't keep quiet any longer. 'Don't you see? Nancy must have *found* them. I told her they'd been stolen and that *I* was suspected as the thief. Nancy was trying to help.'

Miss Kettle turned to Quentin. Her eyes settled on him, glinting and shrewd, as if she was taking in everything about him. He worried that she might even be as observant as he was. Standing up and glaring about the room, he said, 'I can assure you—Miss Kettle, Mr Otter—that Nancy Parker is not your thief. If anything, she has uncovered *the real thief*.'

'Hmm. That's her story, too.'

Beans said, 'Please, Dad, trust Quentin. Please, Miss Kettle.'

'You have my word as a gentleman,' said Quentin, sticking out his hand for anyone who would shake it.

56 NOT MY BOSS

NANCY'S JOURNAL

Who should visit me next but Mr Cosway Otter himself?!
Miss Kettle showed him in. He wasn't angry. His voice was
soft but he had a way of looking you in the eye without
blinking. Which he did while getting me to tell my story.
Miss Kettle would keep jumping in & I never explained it
all. Mr Otter looked vexed with us both.

'Quentin Ives will vouch for you, Nancy Parker,' he said
& then turned to Miss Kettle. 'Can you vouch for Quentin
Ives?'

She nodded—acting v. awkward & twisting her
cardigan. She knows that Lady Sleete won't like this.
Not one little bit!

I never got the chance to tell Mr Otter about Sophie
really being Nesta Vye—cos Miss Kettle announced she
must speak to Her Ladyship right away & Mr Otter said
'I'm coming too. I'd like to speak to her myself!' His voice
was still soft but even so there was STEEL in it when he
said that.

LATER

After some time Miss Kettle came back & marched me
off to the Rose Room where she ordered me to stay put.
She did not menshun Lady Sleete at all—only said she'd

promised the Butler that I would be on my best behavior! I was to do whatever Miss Lamb required & nothing else. Then she went off to fetch her.

Just struck me that if I'm not really a servant here at all—just acting like one—I don't have to follow anyone's orders. Miss Kettle is not my boss. Nor is Miss L. for that matter!

Course I'm grateful to Miss Kettle for keeping me out of Lawyer Hawk's clutches & getting me OFF THE HOOK just now. But I can't stick around waiting for Miss Lamb to come & act all worry-guts again. There's Important Investigations to get done.

Soon as I finish these notes I shall borrow Miss Lamb's hat & coat. If anyone sees me they'll think it's her. (So long as she isn't actually with them at the time!) Thank goodness the afternoon is dark & dreary.

Just quickly post a note for Quentin—then out to find Mr Betts.

Dear Q.

So much to tell you! Tho there's more I must look
into first.

A little bird tells me you
may have heard
something too!!

I know where the d**d b**y is. Vital to investigate
while all are ockupied with Sharades.

Usual place. 9 o'clock. Bring torch.

                                    N.P.

                P.S. Thanks for sticking up for me.

57 BLABBERMOUTHS

NANCY'S JOURNAL

LATER

Had to sneak out thru a boot-room by the Archway Entrance. Snow's been cleared the off the bridge but the moat's still frozen hard. I slipped & slithered over to the out-bildings & found Betts in the garage.

I needed all my DETECTIVE'S CUNNING to get him on my side. My Aunty Bee says Flattery will get you everywhere! so I reminded him who I was & said 'I bet as a driver you see all sorts. You must be a good Judge of ~~Carr~~ Charackter.'

I told him Miss Lamb was such a kind mistress (I did not say schoolmistress!) to a young maidservant like me. She would never dream of overworking me or being mean. (Unlike Lady Sleete herm-herm.)

That's how I got him talking. (Betts must be lonely out here in the yard by himself for he did not stop once I set him off.) He agreed that Miss L. was a nice modest lady not like some people. For ecksample—Mr Grant who acted so frendly but really had his nose stuck in the air. But he liked Lily Lopez. He'd fetched her all the way from Eden Castle. Dispite being famous Miss Lopez did not PUT ON AIRS—unlike that maid of hers who got in a <u>fair old mood</u>

on account of being kept waiting at the station. Said she'd been standing about in the cold for half an hour.

This was Interesting!

'Not the maid who was with her at Eden Castle' he said. 'We dropped her off to catch the London train & collected the other one—the one who's here now.'

So Lily's real maid must have been with her for Christmas & then got swapped for Nesta Vye on the way to Midwinter!

Betts said they talked in funny voices all the way in the car. 'But then that dark-haired maid is French. Suppose that's what they were speaking.'

I know what they were up to: practissing how a French maid would speak. Just like Miss Beaumont got me and Miss Lamb to play-act being mistress & maidservant the night before we came here. But I'm here to help Miss Lamb out—& Nesta Vye is here to steal Secrets & Blackmail people.

While I'd got us chatting so easily I said 'Be lovely when you & Edie are set up in that Sweetshop like you always dreamed.'

His face! I told him Edie & me had become firm frends & she'd let me into their secret. Then I gave him another shock! Said he must tell me what he knew about Miss Lamb & the private investigator. I repeated my Love & Loyalty for Miss L.—how Lady Sleete had been cruel to her & since Doctor James was cut off by the snow there was no one here to stand up for her but me.

(I laid it on very thick—but it worked!)

He told me he was sheltering under the doorway to the Libary when he heard Mr Hawk & the visitor. Arguing. Mr Hawk asked why had he not sent a report like Her Ladyship wanted. The gentleman insisted there was nothing to report. That's why he needed to speak to Lady Sleete IN PERSON—cos the lady in question was entirely blameless. Not a spot on her record to be found. He called her THE EXCELLENT MISS LAMB. Mr Hawk said Her Ladyship would be unhappy with that. Talked about 'not what she paid for'. The other gent declared if she did not like it she must get someone else to look into the matter—but they would find the same.

No wunder Mr Hawk was desperate to find out what I had seen or heard in the Libary!

The one other thing Betts heard was coughing. (Quentin said that too.) Must have been Mr Phipps cos sometimes it got in the way of his words.

I asked if there were sounds of a struggle—or a cry—or a body falling to the floor? But he said No. He was perishing half to death with cold by then so he slipped away home across the yard.

So much for Lady Sleete keeping her servants on a Tight Rein. Both Betts & Edie Little are a pair of blabbermouths! Thank goodness.

58 FEVERISH

NANCY'S JOURNAL

Who did I find when I got back to the Boot-room but Lily Lopez? All done up in furs & trying on a pair of great ugly rubber boots. She gave me the quickest glance saying 'I wonder if these belong to Miss Kettle—or Lady Sleete?'

This was my chance to speak to her alone.

But she carried straight on. 'I swear I shall never speak to Jasper Grant again. He didn't warn me that we'd have to play Sharades. What a Busman's holiday! I'll die if I can't escape for a bit & breathe some fresh air. I'd rather expire in a Snowdrift than spend another moment with all those idiotic —!'

She looked up again & saw that I wasn't who she thoght I was. 'Oh it's Nancy Parker. That's a very fine hat you've got on.'

I swallowed hard & told her Miss Lamb lent me the hat & coat. (Only a small lie.) Didn't know what to say next. Lily Lopez sort of Stops You in Your Tracks. Just like at the Pictures when there's a great big face up on the screen—wide eyes—sweet mouth—perfect in every way—& the whole cinema just gazes back.

Seeing me go blank Lily said something about hoping Sophie's advice was helpful. Helpful!? Salt to get a soup stain out of velvet? That's when <u>I knew that she didn't know</u>. Sophie hadn't told her about SWITCHING THE PAPERS & getting me into trouble.

- Maybe their paths had not crossed yet (easy in Midwinter Manor).

- Or maybe Lily really <u>wasn't</u> mixed up in it.

The blood must have rushed to my head for I blurted out 'Sophie's not really your maid. I know all about Nesta Vye. I can <u>prove</u> it.'

'Did you just catch a chill, Nancy? You're babbling nonsense—& you look quite flushed.'

I wasn't talking nonsense. Seemed like she was just trying to change the subjeck. Thing is (now that she came to say so) I was feeling a bit shivery. Lily jumped up & felt my forehead—held my rist like the doctor does—pointed at my feet which were wet with melting snow. Every bit of my shoes was leaking again & my stockings were soaked.

Before I could help it she'd bundled me up to the Rose Room. Miss Lamb was already there—looking worried—& when Lily explained I was FEVERISH she looked even more so. Lily insisted I rest on the sofa & certainly not up in the maids room which Sophie had complained was v. drafty & cold. Then she nipped out to fetch a ~~Thur~~ ~~Threw~~ Thermom-eter from her room. Told Miss Lamb she never travels without a whole Doctor's Kit. Actresses always live in fear of a sore throat or a cold on the chest!

Soon as she'd gone I told Miss Lamb about Sophie Leblonk & Nesta Vye & the papers & the suitcase. About being locked in Miss Kettle's Eyrie. About how if you went in the bathroom you could hear talking thru the wall & Sophie never used her French voice then.

Miss Lamb just looked at me as if I'd gone MAD.

So I got this notebook out & scrabbled thru it for the clipping of Lily & Nesta to prove it. Couldn't find it! Turned out my pockets. Nothing. Disaster—must have lost it somewhere!!

Miss Lamb shook her head saying Miss Kettle had told her there had been MORE TROUBLE—& how awful she felt bringing me here at all! Now I'd taken a chill and she'd never forgive herself if I got really sick. She insisted on tucking me up in her own bed (not that cramped little sofa. Said she could give the Sharades a miss & look after me instead.

I persuaded her she must not! (I've got URGENT WORK to do!!)

Lily came back & took my Temperchure. It wasn't <u>too</u> <u>bad</u>—but I better keep warm & rest just in case. Miss Lamb nodded & took Lily's arm. 'Let's leave her in peace. We're supposed to be downstairs rehearsing for the Sharades.'

'Lord!' said Lily. 'MUST we?' & Miss Lamb told her yes. Becos she was looking forward to Lily's performance most of all.

So here I am snuggled up in a nice soft blanket. Just written all this down. Dam & blast that my Solid Proof about Nesta Vye has gone! And that Miss Lamb seems to think it's my FEVER that's talking.

59 A GOOD LIAR

NANCY'S JOURNAL

Next thing Sophie was in the room holding up a brown glass bottle. Miss Lopez told her to give me this—her best all-round Cold Cure & how it would perk me up no end. She looked sulky as she said it as if she didn't like Lily Lopez being kind to me. It tasted of Syrup of Figs mixed up with Dr Forrest's Alpine Throat Gargle (which is what Gran swears by in the winter).

Soon as I swallowed it Sophie grinned. Had her hand on the door but I wasn't letting her get off so easy.

'You tricked me! I know who you are. You're not French. You're her understudy.'

She nodded—as if me & her were old pals & I would understand. Said it was just a bit of fun. She wanted to get out of London & Lily wanted company. Even tho house parties can be deadly boring Lily's so obliging she always says 'Yes' to invites. She couldn't bring a frend along without Her Ladyship's say-so. But she could bring a maid.

I said 'Why did you steal those papers? What's it got to do with Sir Marmaduke? Who are you working for?'

She looked blank. Truly as blank as the new-fallen snow outside. 'I've no idea what you're talking about now.'

I was almost taken in. She's a very good liar. The way her face switches to perfeckly match whatever she's saying! But then she's an ACTRESS. A proper one on the London stage. (Even if just an Understudy.)

'I didn't make it up! They were in your suitcase before they were in mine.'

She gazed at me—quite calm. 'Really? No one beleves that but you.' Then she was gone.

I shouted after her 'I know more than you think—' but my voice got all fuzzy & it didn't come out right. Maybe I have got a chill. Feel quite thick-headed & ever so slee

60 CHARADES—PHOOEY!

It was four o'clock. With a heavy heart Quentin found his way to the Oriel Room in the oldest part of the manor house. A large window jutted out over the courtyard, and Quentin could clearly see writing scratched into several of the small glass panes. Everything in the room was dark and heavy: ancient tables with candy-twist legs, dim oil paintings, sofas so deep they might have actually collapsed. In the deepest one Princess Canova was curled up.

'Quentin Otter!' she piped. 'At last. I thought no one was coming.'

Quentin sat down warily on a sunken-looking chair. 'I wonder, have you seen Miss Lamb about, Your Mmmhhnnss?'

Princess Canova shook her ear trumpet as if it must be faulty.

Quentin tried again, pronouncing each word slowly and clearly. 'Miss. Lamb. Young lady. Dark hair.'

The Princess struggled to sit up. 'I've not seen a soul. Everyone's in hiding. It's the charades! I can hardly blame them. We are only here to do what Margery wants us to.'

'Margery?' The Princess pointed her ear-trumpet at him and Quentin repeated, 'Who's Margery?'

'Her Ladyship, of course.' She croaked her creaky laugh. 'She was plain old Margery Smithers before she got her claws into poor foolish Sir Anthony and became a Sleete.'

Quentin had never heard of Sir Anthony. But then the Princess wasn't very reliable with names. She was still convinced that he was an Otter. He said again, 'Margery Smithers? Are you sure?'

Princess Canova's beady eyes sparkled. 'Indeed so. Margery Smithers from nowhere. Such a cunning little gold digger! Determined to bag a fortune wherever she could. Now Anthony is long dead and the fortune is almost gone.' She lay back, exhausted, and sighed. 'And so is mine. Long ago. The dear Prince, and that heavenly castle by the glittering sea…'

'I'm sorry to hear that, Mmnness,' said Quentin absently. His mind was working rapidly elsewhere. If only he could find Miss Lamb. He had even more to tell her now. Lady Sleete had *a past*. A gold digger from nowhere accusing spotless Miss Lamb!

The Princess began polishing the wide part of her ear trumpet with one of her scarves. She muttered something.

'Beg pardon?' said Quentin.

'I said, charades—phooey!'

'I thought she couldn't hear,' Quentin muttered to himself.

'Deaf as a post,' the Princess went on. 'Still know what people are saying, so long as I can see their lips moving.'

Quentin was amazed. Can you indeed? But he kept

this remark safely inside his head. He mouthed, 'I don't care for charades either, Mmmhhnnss. I'm only here because Mummy made me.'

She cackled back, 'And I'm only here because I can't get out of this chair!'

The door blasted open, letting in a freezing draught, followed by Sir Marmaduke Roxburgh. He held Lily Lopez by the elbow. 'Well, well, let's get on, shall we?' he said.

Quentin got his mother's crumpled note out of his pocket. 'I thought, Sir, that Mr Otter was to be in this team—' he began.

'Otter? No, no. Complete change of plan.'

'But it says here in the instructions—'

Mr Roxburgh plucked the paper from his fingers and tossed it into the fire. 'I don't take instructions,' he said, and pulled his chair up close to Miss Lopez.

61 FROM BAD TO WORSE

Things were going from bad to worse for Quentin.

The business with the charades went on for ages, deciding on costumes and what to say and do. Then when he escaped to children's tea he found his mother there at the head of the table. In that American way the Otters had, Scottie was being very polite and charming to Mrs Ives. There was no sign of Beans. Scottie said she was 'in her room', and gave Quentin a fierce look that told him not to ask any more. Miss Kettle, more agitated than ever, put her head into the room to say, 'Can't stop—do apologize—but Her Ladyship needs me.' At least while Scottie and his mother chattered away, Quentin could concentrate on eating; though the sandwiches were all the same kind and the cake was very dry.

When he could get a word in edgeways, he asked, 'Mummy, have you seen Miss Lamb at all today?'

'Of course. We were cooking up our charades together just now. Miss Lamb was so helpful, if a little shy. I heard her telling Mr Grant that she had been walking in the Long Gallery for hours today on her own! Imagine that—when there are so many fascinating people here for company.'

The Long Gallery. They must have just missed each other. If only he'd known. Added to which he'd heard nothing from Nancy. What if she was *still* in trouble?

Quentin retreated to his bedroom, and thought about the Charades. Miss Lamb would definitely be there, and all the other guests, with Lady Sleete presiding. It would be the perfect time to report back to her, and probably the only chance he'd get. A cunning idea was beginning to form.

Someone knocked at his bedroom door. Beans Otter, in a baby blue dressing gown and rabbit fur slippers.

'I came to let you know I won't be joining in with the charades. I shall be in bed with a terrible sore throat.'

'Is that why you missed tea? You sound all right to me.'

'Of course I *sound* all right! I *am* all right. Just not if Lady Sleete—or anyone else—asks.'

'What about Scottie?'

'Oh, they've dug out some genuine ancient armour for him to parade about in, so he's quite happy. What about *you*?'

'What about me?'

Beans handed him a tightly-folded piece of paper. A note from Nancy, one he hadn't seen before.

I know where the d**d b**y is. <u>Vital to investigate</u> while all are ockupied with Sharades.

'Where—where did you get this?'
'The bannister-post. Your hiding place.'

'How do you know about that?'

Beans folded her arms. 'I'm not stupid, Quent. I *notice* things.'

They glared at each other for a moment without speaking.

'N.P. is your friend, Nancy Parker. I'm right, aren't I?'

Quentin gave the smallest nod. He said, 'If she's sending notes, she must be all right. Do you know any more about it?'

'Nancy said the maid who shares her room took the papers. Miss Lopez's maid. Dad and Miss Kettle questioned her but she denied knowing anything about it. Utterly convincing, Dad said. There's no evidence she actually ever had the papers, only Nancy Parker's word for it.'

'Nancy's word?' Quentin spluttered. 'Nancy's word's as good as mine!'

'Dad wanted to question Miss Lopez too, but Lady Sleete won't hear of him spoiling the party. She says he's got the papers back intact, and those involved are only *witless girls*—what could either of them possibly do with such stuff? She's going to talk to Lily privately, to save embarrassment, once this evening's over. That's her way, isn't it? Quietly fixing things behind the scenes.'

'Fixing them to her liking,' Quentin growled. 'I'm going to fix *her*, though, at the charades.'

Beans nodded at Nancy's note. 'Won't you be busy digging up bodies?'

Quentin read it again. Examine a corpse—at dead of night!? He shuddered. Did Nancy really intend that? If so, she could go it alone.

Beans gave him a long look. 'What would Sherlock Holmes do?'

'Oh, blast,' said Quentin, scrambling out of his dressing gown. 'Beans, do me a huge favour?'

'Only if you tell me everything else you overheard in the secret passage. *Every*thing.'

'I will. But you'll have to play charades, whether you like it or not. You're going to make a miraculous recovery and take my place. Say *I'm* ill now. Only not so ill that Mummy runs upstairs to see how I am. Tell her I just want to sleep. Oh, and you'll be needing this.' Quentin stuffed the dressing gown into her hands. 'I was going to wear it as a robe for some stupid play-acting part. We're meant to be Henry VIII and his courtiers.'

'It's much too big.' Beans turned to the window. 'Wait—what's that noise?'

'What noise?'

But they could both hear it now.

'Funny. Sounds just like water dripping.'

'Snow's melting.'

'It's raining!' said Beans.

62 THE CRYPT

'Ready?'

'Ready.'

Or as ready as he'd ever be. Quentin was dressed for exploring: everything dark. His hair was covered by a black wool cap lent by Beans; his face smudged with soot from the bedroom fire. But this wasn't the same as exploring with the Otters. This time they were off to find a body. A *dead* body.

He glanced at Nancy. 'Are *you*? You look half-asleep.'

Nancy shook her head vigorously, just like a horse shaking away a cloud of flies. 'Long story. Think I was given something to make me sleep. Only just woke up in time. But I'll be all right. Let's go.'

They slipped silently into a region of the house that Quentin had never been in before, never imagined. Down dim passageways, under crumbling ceilings, past cramped yards. There were food smells, drain smells, sharp disinfectant and laundry soap. Once or twice Nancy flinched at a sound and flattened herself into the shadows. Quentin did the same.

At long last Nancy stopped in front of a heavy door. 'This is it.' The handle turned. The door swung slowly open.

The only light came from a row of slit windows high on the far side, bleak beams reflected off the snow. The only sound was a relentless drip, drip, drip. It was very cold.

The hairs on the back of Quentin's neck stood up. The door thudded shut behind them. He flinched. Clicking on the torch, he saw stone walls, arches holding up the roof, a bare stone floor. Beneath the windows lay a long table, striped with light and shadows. There was something on it. Lots of somethings, odd heights and shapes and sizes. He squinted, then blinked, trying to make sense of them. The shapes resolved into buckets and bowls and pans, all lined up. Nancy was already walking towards the table, one hand out.

Quentin couldn't do anything but follow.

He could see that the buckets and bowls were in two rows. In between them was one long shape, draped in a sheet. A shiver ran up and down his spine.

Nancy put one hand into the nearest bowl and took it out, wet. 'Snow—and it's melting.'

'Snow?'

'Placed round *the item in question* to keep it cold. Till the authorities get here. Meet Mr Osmond Phipps, Private Investigator.'

'Cripes. You know it was your Miss Lamb that Lady Sleete hired him to investigate? Hoped he'd dig something up to stop the marriage with her grandson. I listened in on her from one of those secret passageways.'

'Did you indeed!? I squeezed the same story out of Mr Betts, her driver. *He* was the person you saw crossing the courtyard in the dark. He'd been earwigging, too.'

Quentin's mouth dropped open. 'We've done some really good investigating, Nancy.'

He saw the flash of Nancy's grin in the darkness. Then she said, 'Now we gotta examine the body. For evidence of how he died.'

'We?' Quentin's insides felt as they had on the car ride to Midwinter Manor.

'It's what we're here for. You can help by shining your light in the right place.'

I can manage that, he thought.

'Stand back.'

Standing *well* back, he held the torch beam high, and—mostly—unwavering.

Nancy took a corner of the sheet and twitched it away.

Cold snow-light fell over a stiff body. Quentin kept his eyes on his own fingers gripping the torch.

'Not much to see,' said Nancy. Her voice sounded fainter than before and just a little bit wobbly. 'No head wound. No—um—holes in his coat-front.'

'Holes?'

'From a bullet. Or a knife.'

'Ohhh.'

'No blood.'

'Good.'

'Well, it's not good, is it? Cos we don't really know what killed him, without any wounds or blood.'

'I see.' Quentin paused. 'Could it be that his heart just naturally gave out?'

'We'd need a doctor to tell us that. And we haven't got one. We'll have to turn him over.'

'Really?'

'Could be wounds elsewhere, you see.'

'Yes.'

'I'll need your help now—your actual help.'

Quentin put his torch down, stepped closer, and took the edge of the sheet from her. Nancy moved a bowl of slushy snow, and then another, out of the way. She grabbed *the item's* coat by its shoulder and cuff, and tugged. Nothing much moved. She tugged again. Still nothing. She leaned right over *the item itself* and heaved at it with all her might.

Something gave. Something slipped, amongst the wet bowls and the dripping buckets. Something slid. A heavy weight fell forward. Nancy's feet, in a pool of water, skittered from under her and the item in question lurched over the edge of the table.

Quentin clutched through the sheet, but encountered a bucket instead of a body and felt it tip up. Icy water deluged him and he leapt away.

The item—and Nancy—hit the ground with a thump and a splash, and something hard as stone shot at Quentin. Was it a bullet? With numb slippery hands he clutched at his chest. A corpse had—somehow—killed him. As he sank to the floor there came a thunderclap and a flash of flame. His last clear thought was, 'Mummy will be so cross about this.'

63 DEMONS OF HELL

NANCY'S JOURNAL

It was TERRIFYING!

There I was lying in a pool of icy-cold water with poor Mr Phipps's dead body right beside me. Quentin had fallen in a faint.

Next there was a crash & a flash & the Cript cracked open! We'd done something terrible—messing with a dead body—& all the DEMONS OF HELL rushed out at us. Monsters—Ogers—Devils—I'd never seen the like before!!

Then a bright light shone in my face & blinded me. One of them said 'Good greef! What have we here?'

The light roamed about—stopped—& was set down. I could see (with aching eyes) that it came from a powerful lantern. A Demon stepped into its beam. A great shapeless body with a shaggy hide down its back—& a huge <u>extra pair of eyeballs</u> on its bald head.

Quentin sat up & stared. I had to admire his nerve. I thoght he was out cold. He pointed straight at the monster and cried out 'I know you! You're Pansy Roxber!'

The monster laughed. Ackcherly laughed.

Quentin said, 'I've seen your picture in the paper. Flying an air-o-plane'.

The monster laughed some more—a big throaty roar like a bear. 'Did they say I crumped it?'

Quentin said 'No. Only that it was your birthday present.'

'Oh well I did smash it up a bit the next day. Not nearly as bad as I smashed the old motor just now. Didn't I James-y?'

My eyes were improving by then & I got up—dragging myself out of the puddle—to see there were only 2 of them. They didn't look so monster-like now. I could make out that the extra eyeballs & bald head were driving goggles pushed up over a leather helmet. The shapeless body was baggy canvas overalls with a nasty-looking fur waistcoat on top. If Quentin was right—& he seemed to be—this was Marmaduke Roxber's girl! The one Miss Lamb was sick of hearing Lady Sleete go on about!!

Next to her stood a gentleman in a hairy tweed coat & hat with about 10 scarves rapped round his neck. The light glinted off his specs so I couldn't see his face well.

'And who might you be?' he asked us.

'I'm Quentin Ives & this is Nancy Parker.'

Must say in a tight skweeze Quentin knows how to speak up. (It must come from knowing your place in the world—& that place not being at the Bottom of the Heap.)

'Well I'm James MacDonald & this is my grandmother's house. What on earth are you 2 young things doing in the Cript in the middle of the night?'

So this was Doctor James! I might have asked him the same thing.

'And who's your frend here?' asked Pansy Roxber—turning the light on Mr Phipps. It seems most odd to call him our frend!

So I took a leaf out of Quentin's book (trying to sound as firm as him). I said we were looking into the suspishus death of Osmond Phipps, Private Investigator—becos no one else would. Becos the Lady of the Manor acted as if it was a trifling annoyance. Becos we needed a doctor & there wasn't one. Becos the orthorities haven't come—the telephones are down—and everyone's TRAPPED BY THE SNOW.

Pansy Roxber put in 'Not everyone! We got here.'

Doctor James added 'Only just.'

Turns out they met at a party in London last night. Pansy said she could see he wasn't in a dancing mood & he explained how the snow was keeping him from Midwinter Manor. 'Just the place I was trying to avoid!' Pansy chuckled. But she fancied an Adventure & bet him a fiver that if anyone could drive him down there it was her. The journey was a little HAIR-RAISING (here Dr James snorted) but they did all right til that bend at the top of the hill where they skidded right off the road & into some trees. 'Only small snappy ones' according to Pansy. They went on foot thru the woods—coming across the Ice House—where James knew there was a service tunnel under the moat with a door into the Cript. (The one Edie Little told me about—I'd quite forgot.)

So that was how they burst upon us—like veritable Demons pouring out of Hell—with Pansy's great big car-lamp blazing in our eyes.

I said 'But now we've got a Doctor. A Doctor who can say if Mr Phipps died of Natural Causes—or Murder!'

Dr James took off his specs & wiped them on a scarf. Tell the truth he didn't look v. eager to get stuck in. Pansy was the one bending over Mr Phipps muttering 'I say!'

Then Quentin piped up—'It spat this out.'

'What spat? Spat what?'

'The body—when it fell.' Quentin held his hand out—flat—with something on it. 'This hit me in the chest. Hard.'

Pansy said 'How in heaven could it cough something up? Does that mean the fellow's not dead?'

'Oh he's very dead' Dr James told us. 'But it's possible a SUDDEN MOVEMENT could give rise to something being eck-spelled.'

Pansy shone her light on Quentin's hand. On to something tar-black & small & round like a ball from an old-times gun. Was this <u>the Cause of Death</u> at last?

'Was he shot?' I asked.

'Not with this' said Quentin—sounding very sure. 'But Beans Otter needs to know about it.'

That's when Dr James announced 'Everyone needs to know!'

64 WHICH MIGHT EXPLAIN

Pansy Roxburgh flung the door open and they crashed into the Great Hall. Quentin, unrecognizable in black cap and soot-smudged cheeks, jostled past Nancy, who was wrapped in warm towels grabbed from the linen room. Everyone looked up. The expressions on their faces! They must think that this was another New Year's Eve tradition: four more outlandish figures dressed up for the charades. Except that these were wilder and wetter and dirtier, and brought the sinister chill of the crypt with them.

Quentin felt a surge of determination. This was *his* moment. No one else was having it. He strode across the floor to where Sir Marmaduke Roxburgh stood, with Beans and Lily Lopez, in a little group around the Princess. They had been interrupted in the middle of acting out their piece.

'Recognize this, Beans?' Quentin tossed a small black object high in the air and caught it again.

Beans stared. 'It's—! Is it really? My Dark Star! My best-ever marble, the one that got stolen?'

'That's what I thought.'

'Where did you find it?'

'Good question.' Quentin held it under Sir Marmaduke's nose. 'One for you, sir.'

'Why, you clever boy!' Sir Marmaduke gave an uncomfortable laugh, tugged at the lace ruff of his Henry VIII costume, and turned to Beans. 'He must have discovered it where I put it—entirely for safekeeping, you understand, Miss Otter—in the tin of cough drops on the library mantelpiece.'

The large and alarming figure in hairy waistcoat and goggles thumped a hand down on Quentin's shoulder. 'Not true,' it roared. 'It was lodged in the gullet of a dead man!'

Various cries, screams, and groans issued from the audience.

The tweed-coated and -hatted figure took off his steamed-up spectacles and wiped them. 'Speaking as a doctor, if a person *were* to mistake a marble for a cough drop, it might possibly end up in their windpipe. Which might explain the corpse in the crypt. Why he's a corpse, I mean, not why he's in the crypt.'

Quentin wished he had on his dressing gown, to give him a Sherlock Holmesian dignity, but it was too bad. He turned to the rest of the room and announced, 'Private Investigator Osmond Phipps is there because he died on business for Lady Sleete—and she wanted to cover it up. He was reporting back on Miss Araminta Lamb, even though there was nothing to—'

'Course there wasn't!' cried Nancy. 'She just wanted to put a spoke in her marrying Dr James.'

'Lady Sleete convinced herself that Miss Lamb was a gold digger. She knows what she's talking about—young

Margery Smithers from nowhere was a gold digger herself when she hooked Sir Anthony Slee—'

But Marmaduke Roxburgh interrupted them, pushing Quentin aside and grabbing the gloved hand of the hairy creature. 'What the devil is all this nonsense?! Is that you, Pansy? How on earth—?'

Quentin stared at the chaos erupting about him. Nobody was listening. His mother had turned crimson and was mouthing silently like a goldfish. His father and Henry Hawk were by the sideboard, helping themselves to glasses of brandy and knocking them back in one go. Miss Kettle flapped about Lady Sleete, who appeared to be having a fit of the vapours, while Princess Canova's eyes twinkled wickedly from under a vaguely Tudor veil. Only Miss Lamb remained quite still on her sofa, with Dr James at her side.

'Brilliant, Quent. You told 'em,' Beans Otter said, with a grin. She stuffed her hands into the pockets of his dressing gown, found the cold toast he'd taken from breakfast, and, having missed her tea, began scoffing it down.

65 DROWNED RAT

NANCY'S JOURNAL

We gave them all such a shock bursting in on their party games like that. Lady Sleete looked like she'd seen a Ghost. Serve her right!

But we weren't the last supprise of the night. For next to stagger in was Betts. His mackintosh coat dripped water everywhere & he was carrying something like a giant DROWNED RAT. I reckernised the fur coat as belonging to Lily Lopez! (But Lily was already there in the room.) The hair that fell out of a be-draggled fur hat was dark. It was Nesta Vye!

Betts chucked his burden down on a sofa where it lolled & wept & groaned. 'Found her halfway up the lane in heap of wet snow. She was nearly a gonner!' he said to anyone that would listen (which wasn't many). 'Had a suitcase with her too.'

Lily Lopez—dressed as an olden-times queen—hurried over and began mopping her frend's face & begging to know what was going on.

I had a BONE TO PICK with the pair them. It was a vile trick of Nesta's to dope me with medicine to get me out the way. I still wasn't clear how much Lily knew.

But Lily was whispering 'What's all this about? What have you done? Where were you going in such frightful weather?'

I wanted to say 'She's stolen your furs—she's run away from a scandal—leaving you to face the music on your own!' Except that Lily really didn't seem to know.

Miss Kettle stepped up by then & was unfolding a scrap of newspaper from her cardigan pocket. The clipping of Lily & Nesta Vye! (So that's where I lost it—must have dropped it in her Eyrie when I was writing my notes.) She said to them both 'Perhaps you would like to explain?'

Nesta Vye sat up & bawled. She spouted tears & tore at her hair. She is a good actress—tho a trifle over the top. 'I did it for love!' she cried. 'For the love of darling Marmaduke. But he refuses to see me! I only took Mr Otter's papers to force him to meet me—he'd be dying know what was in them. Oh, I'm a poor abandoned woman!' Or something like that.

Marmaduke Roxber—looking like a furious Leg of Lamb with that big white frill round his neck—strode over to her

& hissed 'Rubbish. It was nothing but a FLING & over long ago. You agreed to leave me alone & I agreed not to tell about your silly ladies maid game. Nash made that clear to you. Yet here you are.'

Nesta wailed twice as loud—about 'wicked men' and 'cruel Fate'. Lily patted her hand to quiet her.

Lily looked most adorable in green velvet with her long skirts spread out all round (& she knew it!). She took a deep breath—just like she was deciding something—and declared 'It's all _my_ fault.' When they came to Midwinter she couldn't resist telling her frend what she'd learned—all about Mr Otter & his inventions—it was so fassinating. She never dreamed the poor girl had <u>such a crush</u> on Sir Marmaduke that she'd do something foolish like that.

'And it <u>was</u> JUST VERY FOOLISH—wasn't it? Nothing to make a real fuss about. Mr Otter? Sir Marmaduke?' Lily gazed round at them with her big blue eyes. And they gazed back. She'd just cast another spell!

Sir Marmaduke said it was All A Load of Nonsense but he'd be willing to overlook it if Mr Otter would. Beans wasn't happy. She grabbed her father saying 'But she stole your papers & lied about it! And that's another thing Lady Sleete wanted covered up.'

At that Lady Sleete started groaning all over again.

Think I was the only one watching Nesta. There was a very cold look in her eye. Lily may have got her <u>off the</u>

<u>hook</u>. But something tells me Nesta hasn't finished with Marmaduke Roxber yet.

Before anyone could say anything more the Footman burst in. Shouting fit to bust. 'Your Ladyship! Your Ladyship! The telephone's back on. And everyone must get upstairs to safety! For the snow's all turned to floods & THE MOAT IS COMING IN!!'

66 COMPLETED INQUIRIES

NANCY'S JOURNAL

It's taken me <u>days</u> to write those last pages.

So much was going on & I beleve my head was still a bit scrambled from that medicine Nesta gave me. I reckon she did it so I couldn't interfere with her getaway. (It <u>was</u> a sleeping draft. Seems Lily Lopez takes it on her travels when a hard bed or a strange room keeps her awake. I'd rather have a cup of Camomile Tea.)

The Police turned up in the end—but not till next day due to the floods everywhere.

In fact first to arrive was Mr Cosway Otter's own motor car come like A MIRACLE all the way from Seabourne! And who should be at the wheel—with a big grin on his face—but my old frend Alfred Lubbock who works in the garage there? Alfred said the only reason he got thru the flood waters was cos the car had 4 brand-new 'Improved Safety All-Weather Patented Otter' nu-matick tyres. It was the very first try-out of Mr Otter's invention. He & Alfred were <u>pleased as punch.</u> But it meant that the Otters could leave Midwinter Manor before anyone else & I'm sure they were happy to get away.

The Police had questions for Dr James—& Mr Hawk—& the Butler—& Betts—& me! But they never spoke to Lady Sleete for she took to her bed & refused to see anyone.

(Still there—so I hear. Even Miss Kettle's remedies are doing no good.) They completed their Inquiries & 'had no wish to upset her Ladyship any more than was nessersary'. I bet it was Lawyer Hawk who smoothed out that little matter!

It was agreed by the orthorities that Osmond Phipps had choked on a FURREN OBJECT & his death was a Tragic Acksident. Mistook a marble for one of Miss Kettle's Horehound Throat Sweets that Lady Sleete kept everywhere. Lawyer Hawk told the Police that Mr Phipps had a racking cough when they met in the Libary—just before his sudden death!

Must say I was somewhat disserpointed that we did not have a MURDER—& A MURDERER. But then I would not actually wish it on poor Mr Phipps to be murdered in any way. Not when he made all that effort—with a bad cold too—to report that Miss Lamb was blameless.

However we did have A THEFT—& A THEEF. One that got away with it. I've heard from Miss Lamb that Lily Lopez is rehearsing her new play but Nesta Vye will not be her understudy this time. Nesta went down with a nasty bout of Flu after her soaking & is still far from well. I feel a bit sorry for her now. Aunty Bee agrees. 'Running after a horrible man just cos he's rich? Never ends well. Poor & single & happy—that's me!'

The Otters sailed away to America & Quentin Ives must

be back at boarding school by now. And I am home in Bread Street writing this in our kitchen with my feet up on the stove. Who knows what my next job will be? Right now I am just glad to be here.

Only 2 more things to add to this notebook & then it will be full up. (I wunder if I will ever get to show it to that nice Miss Beaumont like she said?)

I must say I was <u>somewhat worried</u> to see what great pals Dr James & Pansy Roxber were. But when I put it to them that Lady Sleete was planning to marry them off together—Miss Roxber gave a great big laugh & thumped the Dr so hard on the shoulder that he nearly fell over. 'Married? To him?! Got more exciting things to do than get married to dear old James-y. Got more exciting things to do than GET MARRIED AT ALL!' So that was all right.

I expect Jasper Grant will put it all in his next book!

'Announcing the engagement of
Dr James MacDonald, Consultant
Physician at the London Chest
Hospital, to Miss Araminta Lamb,
of Blackheath. Dr MacDonald and
Miss Lamb plan to marry at Easter
and honeymoon abroad.'

'ANOTHER IMPRESSIVE WIN!

Miss Pansy Roxburgh (pictured below) came first in the New Forest overland motor trials yesterday. Her astonishing lead over the other vehicles in very ugly conditions was put down to new all-weather tyres from an undisclosed source.

When asked to comment, the incorrigible Miss Roxburgh declared the race, 'Great fun. But not as much fun as when you skid all over the place and end nose-down in a pond!'

A note on Midwinter Manor.

In a deliberate nod to classic crime stories, *Nancy Parker's Chilling Conclusions* features an isolated country house where the characters are thrown together, unable to get away. All the houses in my previous books have come directly out of my imagination. For this one I needed to invent a suitable setting: an old manor house surrounded by a moat, with lots of mysterious nooks and crannies to exploit. So I decided to take a look at Ightham Mote in Kent. I'd visited this National Trust property years before and only had vague memories. But I thought it could prove useful as background research and might give me an extra idea or two. Plus, a nice day out, and cake!

But it turned out to be so much more inspiring than I'd anticipated. Despite the fact that I was there in high summer, and began writing the book in a September heatwave, snowbound Midwinter Manor began to take shape—and its shape was very like Ightham Mote. I gazed at the photos I had taken and kept going back to the guidebook, which included my favourite thing: a detailed floor plan.

Now, separating Midwinter Manor from its real-life inspiration is rather like superimposing one image on top of another and trying to spot the differences. I confess I've played around with the geography and the history of the actual house in order to suit my plot, and invented some things that aren't there. I moved rooms about, dug a tunnel under the moat, and set an ice-house just about where the café is today. The existing tower has gone and instead there's a Long Gallery (possibly the one from Parham House in West Sussex!). But if you visit Ightham Mote you will find the courtyards, the crypt, the Servants' Hall, the Oriel Room, the West Range bedrooms, billiard room and—most important of all— the library, in the right places and perhaps looking a little familiar. I couldn't go into the library while I was there because they were still clearing up the damage caused by a flash-flood after a storm; but I could peer inside. That flood crept into my story, too. You will see the carved Saracen's head where Nancy and Quentin hide messages (though not quite where I've placed it), and spot the centuries-old initials scratched in windowpanes. There's an amazing oversized dog kennel in the courtyard, and I'm still quite annoyed that I couldn't find any way to fit that into my story.

I have no idea if Ightham Mote has any secret passages. None are mentioned in its history, but it's a very, very old house . . . Who knows?

Julia Lee

ABOUT THE AUTHOR

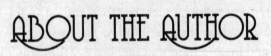

Julia Lee has been making up stories for as long as she can remember. She wrote her first book aged 5, mainly so that she could do all the illustrations with a brand-new 4-colour pen, and her mum stitched the pages together on her sewing machine. As a child she was ill quite a bit, which meant she spent lots of time lying in bed and reading (bliss!).

Julia grew up in London, but moved to the seaside to study English at university, and has stayed there ever since. Her career has been a series of accidents, discovering lots of jobs she didn't want to do, because secretly she always wanted to be a writer.

Julia is married, has two sons, and lives in Sussex.

IN THE NANCY PARKER SERIES

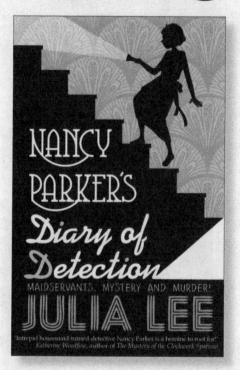

When Nancy Parker gets her first position as a housemaid to Mrs Bryce, it's not exactly her dream job—she'd rather be out solving mysteries. But she soon discovers there are plenty of suspicious occurrences going on beneath her very nose . . . Time for Nancy to set to work not just with her mop but also with her Theory of Detection!

ISBN: 978-0-19-273938-4

IN THE NANCY
PARKER SERIES

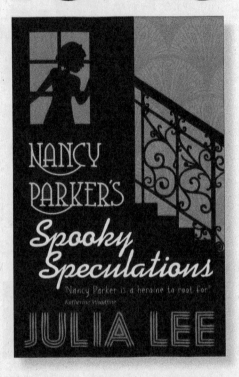

Nancy Parker thinks her luck is in when she finds the perfect job in an old house by the sea. But strange noises and ghostly appearances soon set Nancy dusting off her detective skills. And who better to help than her old friend, Ella Otter? But what spooky secrets will they find as they delve into the mystery?

ISBN: 978-0-19-274697-9

A plucky orphan, a dark family secret,
and a thrilling race against time . . .

Clemency is utterly penniless and entirely alone, until
she's taken in by the marvellous Marvels—a madcap
family completely unlike her own. But it's a surprise
to them all when she's mysteriously bundled from the
house by the frightening Miss Clawe.

Concerned about Clemency's fate, the Marvels
set out to find her. Enlisting the help of some
not-quite-genuine Red Indians, it's a calamitous race
across the country. But Clemency's misadventures are
more dire than her rescuers suspect . . . will they
reach her in time?

ISBN: 978-0-19-273367-2

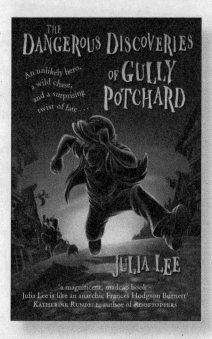

An unlikely hero, a wild chase, and a
surprising twist of fate . . .

'a magnificent, madcap book—Julia Lee is like an
anarchic Frances Hodgson Burnett'
Katherine Rundell, author of *Rooftoppers*

Gully Potchard never meant to cause any trouble. He's
just an ordinary sort of boy . . . at least that's what he
thinks. But when an old acquaintance comes knocking,
mischief and skulduggery follow—and soon Gully
discovers that he has an extraordinary skill which
might just make him an unlikely hero after all . . .

ISBN: 978-01-9-273369-6

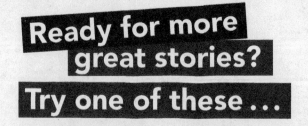

Ready for more great stories? Try one of these ...

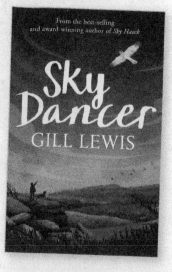